Emily Harvale lives in East
You can contact her via
Facebook, Instagram or Pin

Author contacts:
www.emilyharvale.com
www.twitter.com/emilyharvale
www.facebook.com/emilyharvalewriter
www.facebook.com/emilyharvale
www.pinterest.com/emilyharvale
www.instagram.com/emilyharvale

***

Scan the code above to see all Emily's books on
Amazon

Also by this author:

Highland Fling

Lizzie Marshall's Wedding

The Golf Widows' Club

Sailing Solo

Carole Singer's Christmas

Christmas Wishes – Two short stories

A Slippery Slope

The Perfect Christmas Plan – A novella

Be Mine – A novella

***

The Goldebury Bay series:

Book One – Ninety Days of Summer

Book Two – Ninety Steps to Summerhill

Book Three – Ninety Days to Christmas

***

The Hideaway Down series:

Book One – A Christmas Hideaway

Book Two – Catch A Falling Star

Book Three – Walking on Sunshine

Book Four – Dancing in the Rain

Deck the Halls

Emily Harvale

ISBN 978-1-909917-20-0

Published by Crescent Gate Publishing

Print edition published worldwide 2016
E-edition published worldwide 2016

Editor Christina Harkness

Cover design by JR, Luke Brabants and Emily
Harvale

This book is dedicated to all the members of my newsletter, Readers' Club. Thank you so very much for your support and friendship, and for saying such lovely, kind things about my books. I wouldn't be where I am today, without you. I wish you all a very Merry Christmas.

Acknowledgements

My special thanks go to the following:

Christina Harkness for editing this novel. Christina has the patience of a saint and her input is truly appreciated.

My webmaster and friend, David Cleworth who does so much more for me than website stuff.

Luke Brabants and JR for their work on the gorgeous cover. JR is a genius in graphic design and Luke's a talented artist. Luke's website is: www.lukebrabants.com

My fabulous friends for their support and friendship.

All of my Twitter and Facebook friends, and fans of my Facebook author page. It's great to chat with you. You help to keep me (relatively) sane!

To the members of my new Street Team. I love that you want to help promote my books and spread the word. You're the best!

And finally, you – for buying this book. Thank You. It really means a lot to me.

Deck the Halls

A feel-good festive treat to make your Christmas sparkle

Chapter One

'Unbridled optimism. That's your problem, Harri.' My stepsister, Merrion, grins at me and shakes her head.

I've been telling her how much I'm looking forward to being home this Christmas and spending it with the family. And not just our family but also with my boyfriend, Art, and his family, who'll be joining us for the holidays.

'There's no harm in positive thinking,' I say.

I glance skywards and smile. Tiny snowflakes drift towards the tarmac before they're brutally run down by Merrion's metallic silver Audi R8 Coupé which is so new and shiny, it almost sparkles beneath the glaring lights of the motorway. An early Christmas present from 'a friend', apparently.

'Oh, I'm all for positive thinking,' Merrion says, overtaking several cars that have slowed down to take heed of the flashing warning signs signalling there are roadworks ahead. 'For instance, I'm positive this Christmas isn't going to turn out the way you're expecting it to.'

I wait until we're safely back in the centre lane before giving her a smug smile. 'I don't know about that. It's already started snowing.'

'Yippee!' She gives me one of her looks. The one that leaves me in no doubt she thinks I'm completely insane. But as we're bombing along the M25 at the speed of light, and it's still dark out, she's the one who's insane for offering to come and pick me up. Although I'm extremely glad she did… despite her somewhat questionable driving.

It's a little before six a.m. on a bitterly cold December morning and there are no connecting trains from Heathrow airport to the southeast coast, via Victoria station at this time of day. Especially not on a Sunday. And, in any case, they don't stop at Hall's Cross, the village where our family lives. The nearest station is Eastbourne and then it's a five-mile cab ride inland. I was going to hire a car but Bella, my stepmum, told me not to waste the money.

'Merrion's coming home,' she said, when I confirmed the ungodly hour my flight from Sydney would be arriving. 'She's already offered to pick you up from the airport on her way, and when you're home you can use one of our cars if you need to. There are plenty in the stables.'

That sounds as if we're loaded. But we're not. Yes, we have stables – an entire stable block, in fact – but we only have one horse… and a donkey, and frankly, sometimes it's difficult to tell which is which. And yes, there are plenty of cars also housed beneath the crumbling eaves of the seventeenth-century addition to The Hall, but most of them are ancient – and not in a Beaulieu National Motor Museum-vintage-cars-worth-a-fortune way. More in a rust-bucket-scrap-yard fashion. But Bella's right. Some of them are drivable. As long as you don't plan to drive too far... or too fast, like Merrion is right now.

I check my seatbelt for the umpteenth time. 'Er. What's the speed limit on this motorway? Don't you already have several points on your licence?'

Merrion shrugs. 'No idea. I don't worry about stuff like that.' She beams at me, her perfect white teeth peeking out between luscious-looking lips which *are* worth a fortune.

I'm not joking. Merrion is a model. A lip model, if you can believe that. Her lips are insured for sums that would make your eyes water. They made Bella's water when Merrion told us all, a couple of years ago, before I left for Sydney. "Just think what we could do to The Hall with that kind of money," Bella said at the time, and for a brief moment we wondered if she was considering doing her own daughter harm, so that she could get her hands on the dosh. But Bella wouldn't, of course. She's completely lovely.

The Hall, in case you're wondering, is the ancestral home of – oddly enough – the Hall family, and it sits in several acres of parkland and woods at the edge of the village of Hall's Cross. We own the park and woods but not the village, and the similarity in the names is simply a happy coincidence. The Hall is a Tudor Manor house with later additions, and we got it from Henry V111, who seemed to like giving away fine houses and estates almost as much as he liked chopping off his wives' heads. It's been in our family ever since, despite several attempts by noblemen (and some not so noble) over the centuries to take it away from us. But if what Merrion told me earlier at the airport about the family finances is true, the bailiffs may soon succeed where so many others have failed. Although I'm sure things are nowhere near as bad as she seems to think. She's never understood how The Hall is run or how the family finances work. All she'd say was: 'I have no idea what's going on but money's in even shorter supply than usual and Mum asked me if I could lay my hands on any spare cash as it was getting pretty dire. You'd better ask Dad when you see him. I'll thrash it out with Mum and we can compare notes.' Then, as we tried to cross the road to the airport car park, one of my suitcases fell off the trolley and burst open, spilling the contents – along with most of my underwear into rain-filled gutters. By the time we'd retrieved the sodden garments, the family finances were the last thing on my embarrassed mind.

I hope Merrion's wrong about the money. I want this Christmas to be extra special. I've got some savings of my own and I can dig into those if I need to but Christmas at The Hall has always been such a wonderful occasion and I've built my hopes rather high for this year. The last time I saw all my family was over two years ago at my Bon Voyage party prior to my departure on the 'epic journey'. I was planning to work my way around the world… on a cruise ship before my thirtieth birthday. I made it as far as Australia, where two things happened. I broke my ankle on a bungee jump (don't ask) and I met Art. Ironically, Arthur Camlan-Brown was filming a documentary about how safe adventure sports and activities really are. Or aren't, in my case. He rushed to my rescue. Well, he rushed over to film me writhing in agony, to be honest, but the rest, as they say, is history. Our eyes met (in between my shrieks as the paramedics treated my injury. I don't 'do' pain) and we both knew we were going to get together. I waved the cruise ship goodbye and I've been living in Australia with Art ever since.

We were going to fly home together but Art had a project to finish and I knew The Hall might need a bit of tender loving care to make it look its best, so I came on ahead. He and his family will be joining us on the 23rd and staying until the New Year. That's the plan anyway.

Art's not Australian though. He's from Cornwall where his mum, Dad and sister, Morganna still live. That's why this Christmas has to be perfect. The Camlan-Browns are coming to The Hall to meet me, and Art is coming to meet my family… in the flesh. Well not just 'in the flesh';

we'll all be wearing clothes, obviously. What I mean is, we'll be meeting in person rather than via a laptop screen. I'm nervous about meeting Art's family, if I'm honest, but he seems very keen to make the acquaintance of mine. Especially Dad.

Art says he wants to ask Dad something important but he won't tell me what it is. He says it's a secret and he'll tell me when the time is right. Surely that can only mean one thing. It means he wants to meet the people he's considering having as in-laws and he wants to ask Dad for my hand in marriage. Doesn't it?

That's my interpretation and I'm sticking with it. I agree it's a bit quaint, but he believes the Halls are an old-fashioned family even though I keep telling him we're not, and Art's heritage dates back to the days of the legendary King Arthur – his namesake. Art's sister, Morganna, firmly believes that the Camlan-Browns are descendants of the 'one true King'. I don't have the heart to point out that although some people believe King Arthur is loosely based on a real King, the man himself and his Knights of the Round Table are a myth. Art simply shrugged when I mentioned it to him. "People will believe what they want," he said. "We Camlan-Browns know the truth." Which I must admit, made me think twice about whether he *was* the man I want to marry. Does he actually believe he's descended from ancient royal blood? Albeit, mythological. Next he'll be telling me he's got an uncle called Merlin.

I shift round a fraction so that I'm looking directly at Merrion's profile and it hits me again that she really is incredibly beautiful. How anyone can look that good when they've been up all night – which Merrion told me she has – is beyond me.

She glances at me and grins again. 'I know. I look like I've been dragged backwards through a hedge of holly.'

She preens her silky-smooth blonde hair with the fingers of her left hand then shrugs as if she doesn't care. Which she doesn't. Merrion has never been vain. I'm grateful when she puts both hands back on the steering wheel and there's no point in me telling her how drop-dead gorgeous she is because she's been told that her entire life and she still won't believe it. Instead, I give her a playful poke in the arm.

'I've told Art how wonderful Christmas always is at The Hall and he's even more excited about it than I am.'

'I'm not sure that's possible.' Merrion swerves to avoid a wayward traffic cone and I hold my breath. 'No one can possibly get more excited about Christmas than you. Not even Santa.'

'Well, he is. I've told him all about our family traditions and how wonderful it's going to be. How, when the early morning frost covers the lawns and the scent of pine hangs in the crisp, cold air, we all head out and cut down a couple of Christmas trees from the selection Dad planted as a boy, and gather holly from our park, and mistletoe from our apple orchard.'

'And spend hours removing splinters from our fingers and prickly holly leaves and mud from our clothes. I hope you told him that part.'

I tut and continue. 'How we collect pine cones and pile them in antique bowls with clove-pierced oranges. Or spray-paint them silver and gold. How the north-easterly winds make the endless rows of fairy lights dance in the trees and—'

'Keep us all awake at night, rattling the windows and howling along the freezing corridors.'

I ignore her. I'm on a roll and nothing's going to stop me. 'How we'll stack logs to ensure the fires keep roaring in the massive hearths, in front of which we'll all curl up and drink hot chocolate or Aunt Vicki's heavenly-spiced mulled wine.'

'I think you mean heavily-spiced, not heavenly-spiced.'

'No I don't. It's delicious and you know it. You drink enough of it each year.'

'That's true. But this year she's started making some God-awful cocktail with Reece's help. I haven't tried it yet but it looks revolting.'

'Hmm. A break in tradition. I think that's probably a good sign. It means we'll be making new traditions this year. And Art and his family will be there to share them.'

Merrion laughs. 'You're as nutty as Mum's Christmas cake!'

'Anyway,' I continue. 'I told him about the wreaths we make from holly and Christmas roses entwined with colourful ribbons and which we hang on the blue-painted double fronted doors.'

'Did you tell him it takes six people to open and close those damn doors?'

'Don't exaggerate. It only takes two. He can't wait to see the huge Christmas tree in the Great Hall. I told him it always looks as if it'll topple over any minute from the sheer weight of decorations. And the ancient oak floor, which gleams when it's bathed in the soft, luminous, fading daylight as dappled rays of winter sunshine trip up the oak staircase towards the welcoming warmth of the bedrooms.' I stop for breath and sigh. 'It's going to be perfect, Merrion.'

Merrion snorts with laughter. 'Sorry. Did we just step into one of those Sunday evening, historical melodramas? I hope you didn't tell him there'll be piles of beautifully wrapped presents cascading beneath the tree in the sitting room – because I think we'll be lucky if there's an orange and a nut in our Christmas stockings this year. We'll be lucky if there's a Christmas stocking come to that.'

'Are things really that bad? Or are you exaggerating again?'

She shrugs. 'I don't really know. Mum won't discuss it over the phone – apart from that call I mentioned. That's one of the reasons I'm coming home early. I want to find out what's really going on. I don't think things were so bad when I was home five weeks ago.'

'I'm sure it'll all be fine. And there are worse things in life than a shortage of cash.'

Like dying not long after your thirtieth birthday. I briefly close my eyes as Merrion honks the horn at an articulated lorry the size of Australia. It's hogging the fast lane so she overtakes it using the centre lane. Then, as I peek through half-closed lids, she opens the window and gives the lorry driver a rather unseasonal greeting. Merrion is nothing if not direct.

'It's the season of goodwill,' I remind her.

'Not yet, it isn't. My goodwill begins on Christmas Eve. Besides, the guy's a dick-head. He should learn to drive.'

'Yes. Well. As we were saying earlier. The Hall may be a bit of a dilapidated pile but it won't take long to spruce it up. And it won't cost Dad and Bella an extra penny. I've got some money saved. I'll use some of that.'

Again, that look. This time, Merrion also shakes her head and her silky locks swish around her shoulders.

'You haven't seen the place for the last two years. Seriously, Harri, dilapidated is an understatement. I told you, the place is falling down. It'll take most of the cash in the Bank of England's coffers to keep it standing.'

I frown at her. 'It can't be that bad. It's been standing for hundreds of years and nothing much can have happened to it in just two. I'll admit it's seen better days but it wasn't that bad the last time I was home.'

She tuts. 'You see. Unbridled optimism. You'll be astonished how much the place has changed since you left. Dad's been pouring money into it like Aunt Vicki pours her gin. He took out a loan to repair the roof and chimneys and all those bloody builders did was rip him off. The roof still leaks and the chimneys... well, don't get me started on those. Lighting a fire is like attempting one of Reece's chemistry experiments. Oh – and that's another reason the place is falling down. That idiot brother of ours blew up the kitchen trying to make various chemicals play nicely together, which they clearly didn't want to do. Reece walked out relatively unscathed, but he walked out where the kitchen wall once stood, not via the door... which is no longer there.'

'Oh my God! You're joking. The kitchen?' Now I *am* panicking. Really panicking. How will we cook all the mouth-watering feasts I've got planned? 'Bella didn't mention it. Neither did Dad. Or Ralph. Or Reece.' And that's odd because Reece is always so proud of his experiments. Despite the fact that they all fail. Like Edison, he refers to them as yet another way of successfully discovering how not to do something, rather than another failure, so I'm pretty sure she's kidding. 'Tell me you're teasing me. Please, Merrion. *Please*. Reece likes to tell me what he's recently blown to smithereens –

and he didn't mention the kitchen when I spoke to him three days ago.'

'No can do. But don't worry. It wasn't the main kitchen. It was the old one at the back of the house.'

'You mean the kitchen and scullery? The one that's the best preserved example of a late fifteenth-early sixteenth-century kitchen in the whole of England?'

'That's the one. The one the visitors pay to come and see. But I suppose they won't be. Now it's been blown up, it's not so well-preserved. The woman from English Heritage… or the National Trust or the Tudor Preservation Police or whatever, wasn't happy. Reece would be dangling from a noose if she had her way. Or have been hung, drawn and quartered… like a Christmas turkey.'

I'm sure she's having me on. I'm certain of it. Reece has done some stupid things but for a nerdy fifteen-year-old, demolishing the ancient kitchen and everything in it, is monumental, even by his standards. And someone would have told me if something as dreadful as that had happened. I know they would. I decide to wait and see for myself. I'll probably find it's only the door hanging off its hinges or something, and that Merrion is exaggerating again. She does love to wind people up. Although she doesn't usually do it to me. She's always looked up to me for some reason.

Fourteen years ago when my dad married Bella, her mum, I became the older sister Merrion had always wanted. She's five years younger than me.

Her brothers, Reece – who was a baby at the time – and Ralph, who is the same age as me, became the brothers I wished I'd had, and the sons my own dad had longed for. My mum was ill – on and off – for many years and I was the only child they had during their otherwise happy fifteen years of marriage. Dad met Bella at the hospice where both my mum and Bella's husband spent their final weeks, and friendship blossomed out of mutual devastation. Love and marriage came sooner than either had expected, but their former spouses' cancer had taught Bella and Dad one thing… life is far too short to be wasted. That's an adage the merged families of the Hamiltons and the Halls have come to live by. We take opportunities the moment we can… and worry about the consequences later. Four years ago, Bella and Dad had twin sons of their own, so our family is now truly complete.

'I can't wait to see how much the twins have grown,' I say, changing the subject and getting a little emotional. 'They were in the terrible-twos phase when I left. I suppose they've outgrown that.'

'Yeah. They're even worse now. I hope your future mother-in-law likes kids who do nothing but scream, fight and cause trouble.'

'Don't call her that when she's here, will you? That's just between you and me – and Bella, of course. Until Art actually proposes.'

'My lips are sealed. Seriously though, does she?'

'Like kids? I honestly don't know.'

'Lance says they're like the kid in that horror film, *The Omen*. Only fifty times worse.'

'Lance? Who's Lance?'

Merrion looks astonished. 'Who's Lance? Are you serious?'

'The name rings a bell.'

'I should hope so. He's the guy you've agreed should be employed to do up The Hall.'

'What? I haven't agreed to anyone being employed to do anything to The Hall... yet.'

'Yes, you have. Ralph told me. Lance is his drinking pal. Ralph said you wanted someone to work on The Hall and he told you about Lance. You agreed to take him on and according to Ralph, he's already come up with some ideas.'

I'm confused and say so. 'I remember Ralph mentioning a friend of his who could help do the place up a bit but I don't recall what he said about him other than that. I told Ralph we'd chat about it when I got home and once I'd decided what needed to be done, but that was all.'

Merrion is so busy staring at me, open-mouthed, as if I've told her I've cancelled Christmas or something, that I'm not sure she's seen the long, single lane of queuing traffic, clearly held up by the roadworks mentioned on the warning signs a few miles back. I nod towards the road.

'You might want to slow down,' I suggest.

She doesn't.

'Merrion! Look out!'

She slams on her brakes and why the airbags don't inflate is a mystery as we come to a radical halt, mere inches from the rear end of yet another articulated lorry. This one is stationary and the words: "What do you think of my driving?" are too close for comfort. I don't know about his driving, but I can tell you what I think of Merrion's at this precise moment. At this rate, we'll be lucky if we live to see tomorrow, let alone Christmas.

Chapter Two

Hall's Cross is exactly how I remember it and as we drive through the village of picture-postcard Tudor houses with the more modern Victorian terraced ones added on at one end, my chest fills with a mixture of homesickness and love. Chimneys of all shapes and sizes are puffing swirls of smoke into the cloud-filled sky and even though it's long past sunrise by the time we get here, there's no sign of the golden orb. There are plenty of other orbs though, albeit much, much smaller, hanging from the Christmas tree beside the massive ancient stone cross in the tiny village square.

It's stopped snowing now but the cobbled streets are covered with a smattering of snow and Merrion's car tyres leave the only tracks on the fluffy white blanket as we head towards The Hall.

I'm surprised that no one is out and about but I suppose it is a Sunday morning and it's definitely extremely cold outside. I can still see a few scattered puddles of ice here and there. But it must be getting on now because we were held up by those roadworks for at least three hours and although there are only two hundred or so villagers in Hall's Cross, I would have thought one or two of them had dogs that needed walking. Several houses have lights on; both interior lights and twinkling Christmas lights but the wreath-hung doors are all firmly shut.

We leave the village and I can see the chimneys of The Hall billowing out smoke into the clouds hung low above the trees of the parkland. I want to open the window and reach out and touch the crumbling stone pillars either side of the drive, but I don't. At least the large lamps are still standing proud atop them, but they're not lit; they always were in December, no matter what the time of day.

The Hall does look a little more 'tired' as we approach it and there seem to be a few more cracks snaking up the front walls. Some of the pillars of the colonnade – soon to be strewn with fairy-lights – are cracked and missing one or two pieces in places and the house seems to be leaning slightly to its right side – but that may be my imagination. Most of the roof areas are covered with a dusting of snow but, if my eyes don't deceive me, I can still see there are several loose tiles and... one or two holes.

'Harri! You're home.' Bella rushes down the stone steps at the front of The Hall and comes to greet us as we pull up in the parking area situated at one side of the house. 'And Merrion, my darling. Come and give me a hug the pair of you. Oh, Harri, it's been so long. Forgive the tears. We've all missed you so much.'

'You don't know how pleased I am to be here. In more ways than one.' I throw Merrion a look and she grins in response. 'Merrion's driving is the same as ever.' Bella hugs me in a smothering embrace but I relax into her welcoming arms and let the soothing aroma of her lavender-based perfume seep into my nostrils. 'I've missed you too, Bella. I've missed everyone.'

She finally releases me and stands back a few inches. 'You look... different. Taller maybe.'

'Older. I'm thirty now you know.'

Bella's laughter is like tinkling silver bells and she hasn't changed one bit. She looks exactly the same as she did the day I left. Her white-blonde hair is tied into a classic chignon and I think she's even wearing the same floral dress, although I could be wrong. It was over two years ago after all, but I've got a picture of us all that day etched in my head. And an actual picture on my phone, so I'll take a look later. Not that it matters. Except it sort of does. Bella, like Merrion, has immaculate taste in clothes and this dress looks... well, it looks as though it's seen better days, let's just say.

'Don't be daft, Harri,' Bella says, her eyes sparkling with warmth. 'I'm so glad you liked the birthday presents we sent you. I'm sorry they weren't much but...' She shrugs and links her arm through mine.

'Nonsense,' I say. 'The jumper is gorgeous and so's the scarf. But you shouldn't have gone to the expense of sending anything, especially as you knew I'd be home within a few weeks. And I believe money may be a bit tight at the moment.'

Bella glances towards Merrion who's busy getting our bags and cases from the car. She turns towards The Hall and I have no choice but to fall into step beside her.

'Well, there's plenty of time to discuss all that later. Let's get you inside. You must be exhausted after your journey. Not to mention Merrion's driving. And although I want to hear all your news, if you need to go and lie down, your bed's ready and waiting. Ah. At last. Here's your father. And Ralph and lovely Lance. Will you get the cases, please darlings? I think Merrion's struggling.'

Dad dashes to me and lifts me off the ground in a loving embrace. He spins me round in the air as if I'm six, and he's a fit young man – which I'm not, and he isn't. I see flashes of Ralph grinning at me during each turn, and a raven-haired man, taller and broader than Ralph, with dark eyes and dark looks but about the same age. He's obviously, Lance, but he's not smiling as he walks past us. Until he reaches Merrion and his face comes alive as Dad sets me on the ground.

My head's still spinning when my eyes meet Lance's. The man looks me up and down, then turns his attention back to Merrion. He tosses my large holdall and her smaller one on his shoulder and picks up my case. I'm about to tell him to be careful because the lock's broken from its previous tumble when Ralph grabs me from behind. He throws me over his shoulder like I'm a sack of presents and he's Father Christmas.

'Ralph! Put me down.' Needless to say, he ignores me and bends to pick up another case from the ground.

'Jesus!' he gasps. 'I'm not sure which is heavier. You or this case, Harri. No. You are.'

'*Please* put me down,' I repeat and when he continues to ignore me, I plead with my dad. 'Dad. Will you ask Ralph to put me down, please?'

'Sorry sweetheart. You know I never get embroiled in your rough and tumbles,' he replies, laughing.

To compound my humility, as my torso sways from side to side with each of Ralph's long strides, I can see Lance's legs and his workman's boots following closely behind. I realise the man must have a perfect view of my bottom and I'm glad I wore jeans. I just wish they weren't so tight fitting. I also wish I'd worn a full-length coat instead of the leather jacket that's currently hanging off my back. Oh, the joys of being home.

'You've put on weight, Harri,' Ralph says, adding insult to injury.

I thump him in the stomach but that's not my wisest move as he nearly drops me. I feel a steadying, firm hand on my side and know it must belong to Lance.

'You got her?' His voice is deep and gravelly and ooh so sexy. Damn. I dislike the man already.

Ralph adjusts his hold on me by heaving me up a fraction which causes me to make a sort of grunting sound as my ribcage hits his shoulder. I swear I can hear Lance snigger. Thank God I didn't fart. How embarrassing would that have been!

'Yep,' Ralph says. 'But she weighs a bloody ton. She certainly wasn't this heavy when she left.'

Ralph is definitely *not* going to live to see Christmas. Not if I have anything to do with it.

'Why don't you put me down then?' I hiss, but he still ignores me.

'I bet you're glad to be home,' Merrion says from somewhere close by.

I can't see her but I can hear the laughter in her voice. If I didn't know for certain how much my stepsister and stepbrother love me, I'd have doubts right now.

A loud bang echoes in the air as Ralph bounces me up the front steps – and no, it's not from me. It sounds as if a wall has collapsed and I try to raise my head.

'What was that?'

Finally, Ralph flips me upright and stands me on the stone colonnade. I'll thump him again, once I get my balance.

'Reece,' Dad says, shaking his head. 'We never should have bought him that chemistry set when he was ten.' He's half grinning though, so I'm now pretty sure that what Merrion told me about the old kitchen and scullery was definitely an exaggeration.

'You should see what Lance has done with the Tudor kitchen,' Bella says. 'One would hardly know Reece blew it up just a few short weeks ago. Oh. Have you met Lance, darling? I think you'd already gone off on your travels when he moved to the village. How rude you must think we are, Lance. I do apologise. This is Harri. Harriet Hall. She gets her good looks and lustrous red hair from her dear mother. And my darling Wyndham, of course.'

The colour of my face now outstrips my hair – which isn't really that red these days, anyway. The Australian sun has lightened it by several shades and my hairdresser has added blonde highlights. I still get a little teary-eyed though when anyone mentions Mum, even after all these years, so I blink away any signs of that and manage a smile.

'Hello, Lance.' I hold out my hand for some reason and he stares at it, then up at me, before he takes it in a firm handshake.

'Hi, Harriet Hall. I've heard so much about you that I feel I know you.'

I'm not sure if it's the way his hand's holding mine, or that deep, sexy voice repeating my name, or those dark, brooding eyes, but I can almost hear my ovaries lining up eggs like a pinball machine. The last time I felt like this was when I broke my ankle on that bungee jump and met Art.

Art! The thought of him slaps my hormones down and I can finally respond to Lance's comment without squealing with excitement.

'Really? I'm sorry you've been bored with, no doubt, tales of my stupid antics. I've heard nothing about you, so I've got some catching up to do.'

That didn't come out quite as I meant it but something flashes across his eyes and his mouth twitches at one corner. It's a lovely-looking mouth and it matches the rest of his face perfectly.

'I told you about him only the other day, Harri,' Ralph protests.

'Did you?' Lance is still holding my hand and I quickly pull it away. 'I don't remember that.'

Ralph smacks me on the bottom. 'Too busy planning your wedding.'

He's almost as good as dead now, but I'd like to know who told him about that – as if I couldn't guess.

'Thanks, Merrion,' I say, glaring at her.

She shrugs and slaps Ralph's arm. 'It's meant to be a secret, you utter pea-brain. Don't you dare mention it when her boyfriend and his family arrive.'

Lance frowns. 'You're planning a wedding and your boyfriend doesn't know. How exactly does that work? Or does he know, and you're trying to keep everyone else in the dark?'

I look directly into his questioning eyes, which are nearly as black as his hair and for a second I forget what I was going to say.

'What's this about a wedding?' Dad asks.

'It's nothing, darling,' Bella says. 'Let's all go inside. It's definitely rather chilly out here and besides, we should really go and see what Reece has destroyed this time. I sometimes wish he'd hurt himself – not seriously of course, merely a few cuts and bruises – just enough to make him stop and think about what he's doing. Does that make me a really horrid mother?'

Dad takes her hand and kisses it. 'It's nothing we haven't all considered, once or twice, my darling.'

'I need to sit down after lugging Harri up those steps,' Ralph says, following them as they head inside.

'I need a drink,' Merrion adds, turning towards the front doors. 'And then I'm going to bed. I've been up all night.'

I also turn to go inside but then I remember what I had intended to tell Lance, so I stop.

'I'm not trying to keep anyone in the dark. And I'm not planning a wedding. Secret or otherwise. I merely mentioned to Merrion and Bella that I think my boyfriend is going to ask Dad for my hand when he comes to stay. Ralph, as usual, has got the wrong end of the stick.'

Lance grins. 'Just your hand?' His eyes sweep over me. 'Isn't he interested in the rest of you?'

'Don't be ridiculous. You know perfectly well what I meant. He's going to ask Dad for my hand in marriage. He's going to propose.'

His eyes narrow. 'And you know this… How?'

'Because he wants to meet my family. And because he told me he wants to ask Dad something but it's a secret and he'll tell me when the time is right.'

He tips his head to one side. 'I agree that wanting to meet your family makes it sound as if he's thinking about the future, but it doesn't automatically follow that he's going to ask Wyndham for your hand. Does any man do that these days? Surely it's best to find out if the woman herself wants to be your wife before travelling thousands of miles to ask someone else for permission?'

'He already knows I do.'

'What? You've told him that you want to marry him?'

'No, of course not.'

'Then how would he know?'

'Because… because he knows I love him. And he loves me.'

'Love doesn't always lead to marriage.'

'No. But in our case, it does. Or it will. When he asks me.'

'I see.'

He's looking at me so intently that a strange sensation runs up my spine.

'You're cold,' he says. 'Let's go inside and get Vicki to pour us one of her Christmas Cocktails.'

'Aunt Vicki?' My mouth stays open from the shock of that.

'Y-es. Why the look of surprise?'

'Aunt Vicki hates men. She doesn't even like Dad much and he's her nephew. She barely speaks to Ralph and Reece. And she said she thought the twins looked like slugs as they crawled across the sitting room floor the day I left. If you think she's going to give you a cocktail, Christmas or otherwise, you're in for a surprise. The only thing she's likely to give you are a few sharp words.'

I'm almost laughing at the thought of it but he smiles and my mouth hits the floor – figuratively speaking, of course.

'You're the one who may be in for a surprise, Harriet. Vicki also hates dogs, so I'm told, but she gave my dog, Thunder a bone, fresh from the village butcher yesterday. Perhaps she's mellowing in her old age.'

'Mellowing? If she's being nice to dogs – and you – she must have dementia. That's the only explanation.'

His lips twitch and he steps towards the door, the holdalls on his shoulder and the case in his hand.

'Thanks.' There's a hint of sarcasm in his tone as he passes me. 'I'll try not to take offence at that.'

'Oh! I didn't mean… That is… Um.' I can't think of anything to say so I follow him inside, in silence, trying not to stare at his broad shoulders and incredibly firm-looking bottom.

Art would kill for a bottom like that. Oh God. That's not quite what I meant. Well, you know what I mean. Thank heavens I didn't say that out loud.

What would the man think? What I meant was, Art spends hours at the gym but his bottom doesn't look anywhere near as good as Lance's.

'Harri! Stop staring at my mate's arse,' Ralph shouts, as Lance and I walk into the Great Hall of The Hall.

And now, my humiliation is complete.

Chapter Three

Reece ambles into the Great Hall from the 'modern' kitchen and immediately, panic sets in. I can hear Dad and Bella in there, along with lots of muffled curses. Those are from Merrion.

'Dear God, Reece,' I shriek. 'Please tell me you haven't destroyed the new kitchen as well as the old one. We need to do loads of cooking for Christmas.'

He glances up and his glasses slide down his nose. He peers at me over the rims and a huge smile puffs out his slim, pale cheeks.

'Hello Hairy! No one told me you were home.'

He's not being intentionally insulting and he's genuinely pleased to see me. Reece has called me 'Hairy' instead of Harri or Harriet ever since he was old enough to speak. None of us are quite sure why, but as Ralph and Merrion laughed, it made Reece think it was funny, so it stuck and then it became second nature to him. I gave up asking him to call me either Harri or Harriet – or in fact anything other than Hairy, years ago.

'Hello Reece. I don't suppose you could hear my arrival over the noise of the explosion. Is the kitchen intact?'

Lance turns to me and grins. He then strolls towards the stairs and drops the bags at the foot of them, playfully messing up Reece's already messed up hair with his free hand as he passes.

Reece grins up at him, then at me. 'Of course it is. Excuse me, Hairy, but Aunt Vicki is waiting for this. I'm extremely pleased you're home. It doesn't feel like Christmas when you're not here.'

He walks towards the door to the sitting room and it's only then that I see the contents of the glass jug he is carrying, are not only bright green, but the liquid is also bubbling and smoking.

'What's in that jug, Reece?'

'Aunt Vicki's drink.'

'You're joking! Reece. Sweetheart. I know you think that everything in life is a chemistry experiment but we really don't want you poisoning Aunt Vicki, do we?'

He looks perplexed. 'Merrion said it would be a good idea.'

I roll my eyes and reach for the jug. 'We shouldn't listen to everything Merrion says. I'm sure she didn't mean it. Let me take that from you.'

He holds it to his chest. 'Aunt Vicki will kill me if I don't take it to her, Hairy. She's waiting for it. Truly she is.'

'He's telling the truth,' Lance says. He's leaning against the newel post at the foot of the stairs.

'What? That Merrion said he should poison Aunt Vicki!'

Lance grins. 'I don't know about that – although I wouldn't be surprised. I meant that Vicki's waiting for her drink. That, Harriet, is the Christmas Cocktail I mentioned. It's not poison. Although, depending on the amount of it you drink, it is pretty lethal. And you mustn't drink that bit at the bottom.'

'But… it's green. And it's bubbling and smoking like a chimney!'

'I know. It's gin, crème de menthe and Vicki's secret ingredient which only she and Reece know. The stuff that causes the bubbling and smoke is dry ice.'

'Dry ice! That *is* poisonous.'

Reece grins. 'Only if you consume it – and we don't. It floats to the bottom and we leave it there. This is food grade, too. Aunt Vicki orders it via the internet. It's next day delivery.'

Lance nods. 'It's true, Harriet. And the cocktail is delicious. You'll see when you try it.'

'Thanks. But no thanks. Okay, Reece. Take it to Aunt Vicki. And tell her I'll be in to see her in just a moment.'

Reece smiles and continues towards the sitting room as I head towards the kitchen.

'If Aunt Vicki dies,' I say to Lance. 'It's on your head. I'm going to check on the kitchen.'

He nods and grins. 'I'll go and taste it before she does, in that case.'

He moves to follow Reece, who turns and calls me as he reaches the sitting room door.

'Hairy. I didn't blow up the kitchen, truly I didn't. But there's a tolerably high probability that a new oven may be required.'

Reece opens the door and disappears, and Lance throws back his head and laughs.

'If I ever have a son,' he says, 'I want him to be just like Reece.'

The man may be gorgeous, but he's clearly as mad as they come. And the least likely-looking man to drink cocktails – green and bubbling or otherwise. I wonder if he's gay but immediately dismiss that notion, recalling the way he looked at Merrion. But why his comment about having a son sent tingles to areas of my body that I didn't know could tingle, is beyond me. He likes green cocktails and trainee mad scientists, for goodness sake. I'm not sure what I'd do with a man like that.

And anyway, I'm in love with Art. Who thankfully, isn't in the least bit crazy.

Chapter Four

Fortunately, the damage to the oven doesn't appear to be as bad as I'd expected – according to Bella.

'With a thorough clean and some repairs here and there, it'll be almost as good as it's always been,' she says.

I've long admired her optimism. It's even more unbridled, as Merrion would say, than mine. The 'good as it's always been' remark gives away the fact that this oven, like virtually everything else in The Hall (with the exception of the residents... apart from Aunt Vicki, who's ninety if she's a day) is pretty old. Mum made her famous Christmas biscuits in that oven, and she's been gone for fifteen years. It was old even then.

'Isn't it about time we got a new one?' Merrion asks, pouring herself a glass of champagne from a bottle she's pulled from her Mansur Gavriel Bucket Bag and offering the bottle to Bella, Dad and me.

Even though my watch is still on Australian time and I've lost all track of it anyway – time, not my watch – I'm pretty sure it's a bit early in the day for me to have a drink. I know we were held up in that traffic queue for over three hours and the journey from Heathrow to here takes around two and a half on a normal run, but it can't be later than eleven-thirty or twelve noon. Aunt Vicki and Lance are also drinking cocktails, I realise, so clearly either everyone is this place has lost all concept of time, or they've become rather more keen on alcohol than they were two years ago. I'm actually glad that Dad and Bella decline and I do the same.

Merrion shrugs. 'More for me.'

'We can't afford a new oven, darling,' Bella says. 'Not right now.' She glances at Dad who lovingly smiles back.

I see this as an opportunity to broach the subject of the family finances.

'I couldn't help but notice that The Hall's exterior is looking a little more... weather-beaten than it did two years ago.'

'Aren't we all, sweetheart?' Dad replies.

'Wait until you see the rest of the interior,' Merrion adds. 'The Queen's Room is looking particularly... weather-beaten. But as the rain's been pouring through the ceiling for months now and the only thing the windows keep out is the warmth from the sun, that's hardly surprising.'

'Merrion!' Bella snaps, and that does surprise me. That's something Bella rarely does. 'Harri's only just arrived, darling. Let's wait until she settles back in before we drown her in a litany of The Hall's… issues.'

'Um. I was hoping that Art's parents could stay in the Queen's Room. Is water really coming in?'

'Why don't you believe anything I tell you?' Merrion asks.

'I do. But you are prone to exaggerate.'

'Yes, Merrion, you are,' Bella agrees.

'Well, I'm not this time and the sooner Harri knows what she's up against the better.' Merrion clearly needs sleep. She's becoming overwrought. 'That goes for the rest of us,' she continues. 'Perhaps it's time we sat down and had a serious discussion.'

It seems Merrion's also changed tack and instead of having a word with Bella later, she wants to get things out in the open right now. I'm all for that.

'I think it would be good for me to… catch up with what the situation is regarding family finances,' I suggest. 'Especially as my boyfriend and his family will be arriving in a matter of days and I was planning to put on a few big festive feasts and make The Hall look like something out of a fairy tale. It's important that I make a good impression.'

Dad sighs. He drops onto a chair and Bella squeezes his shoulder.

'Things are not looking terribly rosy for the Hall family finances at the present time,' Dad says. 'Some cowboy builders robbed us blind, so to speak and the last two winters here have been brutal. I suppose I shall have to finally accept that the place is falling down around our ears. I'm not sure what's to be done, sweetheart.'

'And that's without the help from Reece,' Bella says, trying to lighten the mood.

I pull out the chair nearest to Dad and sit down, taking his hand in mine.

'I've got some money. I can help out. It won't take much to do the place up a bit, surely? I know we won't be able to do anything major but we must be able to shore a few things up, and stop a few leaks, if it's really as bad as that.'

I can't quite believe it. I've never heard Dad talk like this. He loves this place. We all do. Even Merrion, as much as she moans and groans about it. Yes, it's definitely deteriorated a little since I last saw it but not enough to cause such melancholy, I wouldn't think. But what do I know? I've lived in this crumbling pile all my life until two years ago, and for as long as I can remember, it's looked as if parts of it might collapse at any moment. But it never has.

'That's kind, sweetheart, but I'd rather you didn't spend your money on The Hall. It's become a bit of a yawning pit. We've been wondering whether it might not be wise to take one of the offers we receive to buy the place – although even they are few and far between these days.'

'No Dad! Don't say that.'

'Don't say what?' Ralph strolls into the kitchen and spots the champagne. 'I'll have some of that, please. Why is everyone looking so glum? It's almost Christmas and I thought Harri's homecoming was supposed to be a happy affair.'

'It is,' Dad says, smiling lovingly at me as Merrion pours a glass of bubbly and hands it to Ralph.

'Then why the gloomy faces?' He raises his glass to me. 'Welcome home, Harri. May you never leave again.'

'She won't be able to afford to leave,' Merrion says.

'Of course she will.' Bella marches towards the kettle and switches it on. 'She's very sensibly bought a return ticket. I'm making a pot of tea. That'll put a smile on our faces, and then we'll have some lunch. We may be poor but we're not destitute.'

'Yet,' Ralph says.

'I could sell my new car.' Merrion's eyes brighten. 'That should buy a few turkeys and seal a few holes.'

'Wasn't that a present?' I ask.

'Yeah. But it's no different from taking back all those awful jumpers Aunt Vicki buys us every year and exchanging them for something we actually like. I'll take the car back and exchange it for cash. I like cash. Besides,' she says, refilling her glass. 'It's not as fast as I thought it would be. They make one with a bigger engine, I believe. I'll ask for that one for my birthday.'

The very thought of that fills me with dread. The one she's got would thrill a Formula One driver.

'And,' she continues, clearly thinking that some of the financial burden will be lightened. 'I should be getting paid soon for the lipstick commercial I just did. That'll add a few grand to the coffers.'

'Have you told them about the baby?' Ralph asks, after taking a sip of champagne.

I stare open-mouthed at Merrion. She shouldn't be drinking if she's pregnant. Then I realise it's not Merrion Ralph's looking at and that my stepsister looks just as astonished as me. Ralph's looking at his mum and he glances at Dad when she doesn't answer.

'Oh. Was that supposed to be a secret, too?' Ralph says. 'I think I'll go and see what Lance is up to.'

He hurries out and the kitchen door slams behind him. The door swings wildly on loose hinges before crashing to the floor.

Reece stands a few feet from the threshold holding an empty glass jug, and looking as surprised as the rest of us.

'That had nothing to do with me,' Reece says.

And for some reason, we all burst out laughing.

For once, it was Ralph, not Reece who dropped a massive bombshell. It seems there's going to be another new member of the Hall family and just as that news is sinking in, the four-year-old twins come thundering down the stairs.

I hadn't realised such small children could make so much noise.

Chapter Five

'Hello. My name's Theo and I'm four years old.'

He stares up at me and he looks so much like Dad that a lump sticks in my throat. His twin pushes him and a small fight breaks out but just as I'm about to stop it, they stop and grin cheekily at one another, then up at me.

'I'm Thor,' his brother says. 'It's short for Thornton but I like Thor. Thor's a god. I'm the olderest son.'

'Eldest son,' Merrion says. 'By two minutes.'

Thor beams at her. 'That's a long time.'

'I want to be like Reece and blow things up,' Theo informs me. 'Will you help me write to Santa? I can't spell that kemstry thingy and Mummy says I can't have one till I can spell it right.'

'I want one too,' Thor adds.

'I think Mummy is quite right,' I say. 'You're too young for a chemistry set at the moment.'

'We're four!' They stamp their right feet at the same time and fold their little arms across their chests but they're not quite able to cross them, it seems. Then they grin.

'When we're five?' Theo asks, looking at Bella.

'Perhaps, darlings.'

I bend down to meet them at eye level. 'Do you know who I am?'

They look at one another, then back at me.

'Course we do,' Thor says. 'You're our sister Hairy from Oz. Where the wizard lives. You're here for Christmas. Did you bring us presents?'

It seems another member of our family will be calling me 'Hairy' unless I can stop it before it takes hold.

'I want a kangoo,' Theo demands. 'Did you bring us a kangoo?'

'No. I'm sorry. We're not allowed to bring kangaroos to England.'

They look disappointed.

'What did you bring us?' Thor asks.

Bella tuts. 'You know better than to ask that question, darlings. Harri's tired after her long journey. Why don't you go and play outside for a while before lunch?'

'Stay away from my car, urchins,' Merrion tells them.

They look at one another, giggle and dash towards the front doors.

'Can they open the doors?' I ask, bearing in mind I can't, without help.

'No,' Merrion grins, 'but they'll spend hours trying. I'm going to bed for a few hours.'

Bella looks surprised. 'Don't you want lunch?'

'No thanks.' She lowers her voice and gives Bella a quick hug. 'I do want to hear all about the new baby though. I can't believe you kept that from me. But I'm so tired I don't think I can stay upright for much longer.'

'I didn't keep it from you, darling. I only found out yesterday afternoon. I'd had a few tests because I've been feeling a little under the weather and Andrew Balfour came round to tell us he'd got the results back. We were all as astonished as you, believe me. Ralph only knew because he barged in on us – like he does – when Andrew was in the middle of telling us.'

I still can't believe the news. 'When's the baby due?'

'June,' Dad says, getting to his feet and kissing Bella briefly on the lips. 'Sit down, darling. I'll make the tea.'

'And I'll make lunch,' I say, realising that Bella needs to rest. She's fifty years old, for heaven's sake.

'Please don't fuss,' she says, but she sits down willingly. 'Let's just have soup for lunch. That way we won't have to clean the oven. We can make it on the hob.'

'Oh. I'll have some soup,' Merrion says. 'I make a killer chilli, cheese and cauliflower soup. Let me help.'

Her exhaustion is completely forgotten and life at The Hall suddenly feels just like it did the day I left. Except it isn't, and I have the strangest feeling that it might not be, ever again.

Chapter Six

Lance doesn't join us for lunch.

'I'm meeting a guy at the pub who may be able to get his hands on some roof tiles for next to nothing,' Lance informs Dad. 'It was good to finally meet you, Harriet.'

He walks towards the front doors after temporarily fixing the kitchen door back on its hinges. I follow him and see the twins are still attempting to open one of the double doors. They are stabbing at the bolt with the sword from the armour of one of the two Knights standing either side of the entrance. It takes both boys to hold the sword upright.

'Oh, good grief.' I run to them to remove the life-threatening implement from their tiny grasps but Lance gets there first.

He grabs the sword and pretends he's going to fight them with it, which naturally brings squeals of delight to their lips as they duck and dive his playful thrusts.

'Be careful,' I say. 'That thing's dangerous.'

Lance glances at me and replaces the sword in the Knight's silver-plated, armour gloves.

'We mustn't play with armour or swords,' he tells the twins.

They look a little despondent until he picks them up, wraps his arms around each of their waists and places them either side of his body. He spins around a few times and makes the noise of what I assume is supposed to be an aeroplane engine as they scream with excitement. When he finally puts them down, they both run around the Great Hall with their arms spread out like wings, trying to emulate the noise Lance was making.

'May I have a quick word, please?' I ask as Lance looks in my direction.

His dark brows furrow but his lips twitch. 'Hmm. That sounds as if I'm going to get a telling off.'

'No. And thank you for removing the sword from their clutches. They could have done themselves some serious harm.' I nod towards Theo and Thor.

'It's a good thing you didn't see Thornton with my hammer the other day then,' he says, using Thor's full name. 'He asked me if it would smash Theo's head to bits. Don't look so horrified. When I told him it would, but it wasn't nice to smash people's heads to bits, he swung it around and dropped it on my foot.' He glanced down at his heavy-duty boots and grinned. 'Steel toe caps. So what did you want to have a word about?'

'Oh. About this place. I wanted to spruce it up a bit over the next few days, if that's possible. Ralph recommended you and I understand you've already done some work on the Tudor kitchen and scullery at the back of the house.'

He nods and grins. 'Ralph mentioned that you'd like a few things done. Titivating, he called it.'

'Oh, did he? Well, it's a bit more than that. I want the place to look thoroughly festive, warm and welcoming.'

He nods again. 'Titivating.'

I'm a little irritated by that and I harrumph rather loudly. In a slightly cooler tone I continue: 'The thing is…' My voice trails off as I'm not sure how I should word this. He seems rather friendly with my family and I know he's been pals with Ralph for some time but I know nothing about him and I'm not sure I want him to know about the dire financial position my family is currently in, in any case.

'Money's pretty tight,' he says, reading my mind.

'Well yes. It is. I've been saving like Scrooge, so that money should pay for a few things. Um. Do we owe you for the work you've already done? Or did you get payment upfront?'

His frown deepens and creases appear at the sides of his dark eyes.

'I'll happily discuss a price with you for anything you want done, but the cost of the work

I've done so far is between me and Wyndham. If he chooses to tell you about our arrangement that's up to him but I don't divulge one client's contract price with another.'

'But… he's my dad.'

'And he's my client.'

'He won't mind if I know.'

'Then ask him, not me.'

'Why are you suddenly being so… so… aggressive?'

'I'm not being aggressive.'

'Yes, you are. I ask you a simple question and you bite my head off.'

'You asked me a question about one of my clients. I don't discuss my clients' business with anyone other than that client.'

'Good grief. You're a builder, not a high-flying lawyer or… or businessman or something.'

'Ask your dad, if you really must know.' He turns and yanks open one of the front doors. 'But I really don't see how it concerns you. You don't live here anymore and you'll be flying back to Australia the moment the decorations come down.'

I'm not sure what surprises me the most. His sudden change in attitude or the fact that he can open the front door all by himself – and only using one hand.

Chapter Seven

'Now that's a man one shouldn't mess with.'

I pull myself together and ensure there's a smile on my face when I turn towards Aunt Vicki.

'I have no intention of messing with him. But if he thinks he can speak to me like that, he's got another think coming. Anyway. How are you, Auntie? It's so good to see you again.'

I'm a little surprised to see that she – like Bella – doesn't seem to have changed much at all in two years. She looks like that Dowager Countess from the *Downtown Abbey* TV series, and always has; the only differences being that the grey dress she's wearing only reaches to just below her knees, not her ankles and she wouldn't be seen dead using a walking stick no matter how unsteady on her feet she becomes.

Her beady eyes narrow. 'A lot better for finally seeing you, Harriet dear. A little annoyed that I've had to struggle out of my comfy chair to come and find you though and if you're going to call me

'Auntie' I'll return to it directly. I'll tolerate Aunt Vicki, as I have for years – although you're well aware that I'd prefer Victoria, but if you start calling me 'Auntie' at my age, you can get on the next flight back to Australia.'

'Apologies, Aunt Vicki.'

'Accepted.' She nods and finally smiles warmly. 'Now come over here and give me a hug. I've missed you, child, even more than I thought I would.'

I do as she says, and realise she's far more spindly than she was. I'm slightly worried that her bones may break if I squeeze her too tightly. She smells of soap and of lilac, which I know has been her signature perfume for her entire adult life.

'Call that a hug?' Aunt Vicki eases herself away from me and links her arm through mine. 'I may have one foot in the grave but they won't be getting the rest of me for many years yet. Unless that stepmother of yours carries on the way she's going. I hear we're having soup for lunch. Soup! It's Sunday. The prodigal daughter's come home and instead of fatted calf for Sunday lunch, we're having soup.' She shakes her head and flicks her hand ahead of us as if she's telling me we're moving forward.

I know she loves Bella as much as I do, so I don't comment on her remark other than to say: 'I'm hardly a prodigal daughter, Aunt. And we're having soup because there's been a bit of an accident with the oven.'

She cackles like the wicked witch of the west and I can feel her body shaking like my smart phone when it's set to 'vibrate'.

'One day that boy will blow us all up in our beds. But I suppose there are worse ways to go. Did you hear what he did to the Tudor kitchen and scullery?'

'Yes. But I haven't seen the damage yet.'

I make a mental note to go and look but she must be reading my mind.

'No point in going to look. Lance has been working day and night and you wouldn't know anything had happened. He says he needs to source a few replacement parts, or failing that, replicas for some of the fixtures and fittings, but even those so-called experts can't tell what's original and what Lance has done. That man has skills, my dear. He's not merely a delight for these old eyes to look at.'

'I think he also has a rather high opinion of himself.'

'Would you prefer him to have a low opinion? There's a great deal to be said for one having self-confidence.'

'Not when it borders on arrogance. How long has Ralph known him? He seems exceedingly 'cosy' with everyone. Even with you, which frankly, I find the most astonishing. You usually have no time for the male of our species. And he walks around as if this place is his second home.'

She nudges me with her elbow. 'No need to get all high and mighty about it, my dear. Lance has been like a breath of fresh air for me. He's changed my views on many things. And he's helped your father out of one or two… shall we say, potentially unpleasant situations.'

I don't like the sound of that.

'What do you mean? What sort of "potentially unpleasant situations" could Dad have got himself into? Financially unpleasant, do you mean?'

She stops and looks me directly in the eye. 'Wyndham was in an unpleasant financial situation the moment he inherited The Hall, my dear. It certainly hasn't improved over the years – despite the hordes of paying visitors tramping all over the Persian rugs like unfettered cattle.' She shakes her head and pulls a face as if she's eaten something exceptionally disgusting… such as a live insect. 'No. Your father, somewhat foolishly, borrowed money from the sort of low-life hoodlum one should never have dealings with, no matter how desperate one is.'

'Oh my God!'

'To compound the problem, he had little alternative it seems but to employ the so-called builders this particular piece of pond-scum recommended. Needless to say, it did not have a happy outcome and when Wyndham was 'asked' to repay the loan – which had grown out of all proportion to the sum borrowed – he could not. That was how Ralph met Lance.'

'What? You're telling me that Lance is some sort of… thug! A loan shark's heavy-man?'

She tuts at me and sighs. 'You're evidently not listening, Harriet. Of course Lance isn't a thug. Quite the opposite. Ralph was accosted on his way home from the village pub one night and fortunately for us all, Lance stepped in and together, he and Ralph saw the scoundrels off.'

I really can't believe what I'm hearing. When I left The Hall, the village of Hall's Cross and the village pub, The Cross in Hand, were a haven of peace and tranquillity. Now it seems the place has become home to loan sharks, cowboy builders and gangsters' heavies. It's almost laughable. Except it isn't very funny. It's actually deadly serious.

'I'm afraid to ask what happened after that. Does Dad still owe the money?'

'Not to those unsavoury characters, no. Lance has friends in the City who, unlike those silly High Street banks, who all refused to advance additional sums, are bright enough to see the potential of The Hall with regard to foreign investors. They all want a tiny slice of an English stately home and to take tea with the English aristocracy.'

Now my head is spinning. Lance is not only some sort of hero, he's also connected with the City's movers and shakers. Added to which, the Hall family now has pretensions of grandeur.

'But we're not part of the English aristocracy and never have been. We don't have a title or even a coat of arms. We just got lucky because a randy old King decided he wanted to have a romp or two between the sheets with one of our ancestors, whose silk merchant father was greedy enough to see where that could lead and reckless enough to risk his head to ask for this place.'

Aunt Vicki frowns. 'But not brave enough to insist on a baronetcy to go with it.'

I've seen the portrait of this ancestor's daughter. It hangs upstairs in the Long Gallery – which isn't actually that long compared to many – and the daughter wasn't that beautiful. Although the whole episode disgusts me, women were pawns in those days and our ancestor knew his daughter's 'value', and also where to draw the line.

'I think he knew that Henry could easily look elsewhere and decided to stop while he was a head.'

'And still had his head.' Aunt Vicki shakes hers. '*We* know we're not aristocrats, my dear, but many of those foreigners don't and The Hall was once as stately as many. The fact that it's falling down seems to add to the appeal. The land is probably worth more without the house these days. Perhaps Wyndham should simply let Reece blow it up, and sell the land.'

'Aunt Vicki! No. Don't say such things.'

'Oh really Harriet,' she snaps. 'You've obviously lost your sense of humour under that Australian sun. You know as well as I that your father would die before he'd see The Hall leave this family, despite anything he says about selling. It's such a pity there are no randy old Kings as you so respectfully referred to His Majesty, around these days. Merrion alone could 'pay' for the house to be rebuilt. And you, well… you're worth much, much more.'

'Not to a randy old King I wouldn't be. I'm thirty now and I've never looked anything like as gorgeous as Merrion. Dad might get the stable roof repaired in exchange for me, but that's about it.'

Aunt Vicki cackles again. 'Don't undersell yourself, my dear. You have certain charms that Merrion will never have, no matter how stunning she may be.'

'Hmm. They're well hidden if I have. So are you saying that Dad now has loans from these foreign investors? They don't actually have shares in the place, do they? And is everything settled with the thugs?'

'No one has shares, only mortgages, and as far as I'm aware the thugs have moved on. Lance also "knows people who know people" to use his own words, who were able to persuade the low lives not to pursue the matter further. But you'll have to ask Lance, if you want precise details.'

There's no way I'll be asking Lance, bearing in mind his reaction to my earlier enquiry. I'm not sure I like the idea of my family being in such close cahoots with a man who knows both City high-flyers and… undesirables, shall we say? I wonder who he really is and where he comes from. I'll have to find out what Ralph knows about his pal, although as my darling stepbrother seems to go through life as if he's in another world, half of the time, he probably won't know much more than what the man drinks.

'What I don't understand, Aunt, is why I'm only hearing about all of this now. We all speak via Skype or FaceTime every few days and yet I've heard none of this. Nothing about the declining finances. Not a whisper of the potentially life-threatening situation. Not even the cowboy builders. Or Reece's demolition of various parts of this house. Why is that?'

'None of us wanted to worry you, my dear. What could you have done about any of it in any event? You live thousands of miles away, and if what Merrion tells me, is true, you won't be returning to live at The Hall again. You'll be setting up home with your husband – wherever that may be. I suppose we all feel you've…moved on. That The Hall is no longer of concern to you.'

That's almost exactly what Lance said, which annoys me.

'Just because I no longer live here doesn't mean I don't still think of The Hall as my home. My real home. I'll always be concerned about it and everyone who lives here. I want to be worried. I want to be concerned. I want to be involved. I want to know what's going on.'

I harrumph and attempt to regain my composure as Aunt Vicki scrutinises me with her beady, watery eyes. Are those tears? I can't recall the last time I saw tears in Aunt Vicki's eyes. Oh yes, I can. It was at Mum's funeral. Oh – and when I left for Australia.

'I suggest you tell your father and Bella that. Now tell me what you're planning for Christmas. It's so good to have you back. Christmas simply isn't Christmas when you're not here. We need to make this one special.'

'I couldn't agree more.'

That's also what Reece said and now I'm really starting to feel the pressure. It seems I'm not the only one expecting big things this Christmas. I'd better get a move on.

Chapter Eight

I spend the entire afternoon making lists. Other than the bedrooms, dressing rooms and bathrooms of my family members, and Dad's study, I walk in and out of every room in The Hall and make a note of all the things requiring attention.

After filling the equivalent of eight pages of an A4 sized notebook on my iPad, I decide to make a *new* list. I go through my first list ignoring anything that I consider is not of the utmost urgency.

Having only reduced the page count by five, I come to the conclusion that Merrion and Dad are right. The place is falling down. I don't have enough money to pay for all the items on the first page, let alone those on the other two, bearing in mind that I've got to buy everything we'll need to celebrate Christmas. That means new Christmas decorations, including Christmas lights; we'd been dragging out the old ones year after year and they were looking pretty ancient even before I left. We'll also need crackers and then there are all those additional festive touches like reindeer embossed napkins – yes, every home should have them. Not forgetting the presents for my family, and for Art's, as well as enough food and drink to ensure the Christmas spirit lasts until New Year. After that we'll have to starve and even Aunt Vicki will consider soup a luxury.

It's clear that Dad and Bella don't have any spare cash to pay for even one bit of this and I now feel incredibly guilty for only letting them know a few weeks ago that I would be coming home this Christmas – and that Art and his family would be joining us for the holidays.

It's not entirely my fault that I sprang it on them at such short notice. It was one of those spur of the moment things, and to be quite honest, when Art suggested it, I thought he was joking. We'd been planning to come home next summer and 'do the rounds' and that's what I was saving towards. We'd spend some time with both our families and perhaps even pop across to Paris for a romantic weekend.

'Why don't we bring the whole thing forward,' Art suggested, one particularly hot weekend a few weeks before my birthday. I like the idea of spending Christmas in the cold again. It's been so long since I've seen snow.'

'There's no guarantee you'll see snow if we go home for Christmas,' I replied. 'Rain – yes. Snow – doubtful.'

I suppose me going on about how much I wished my family could be with me for my big 3-0 and how much I was missing them, made up his mind. Three days later, over a bottle of chilled white wine and barbequed shark steaks (no, not from sharks he'd caught earlier) he announced that we should definitely go home for Christmas and that he'd pay for my ticket as my birthday present. I was pretty impressed, I can tell you. I thought he'd just be taking me out for dinner to celebrate my big day, not paying to fly me half way round the world.

He gave me one of his extremely sexy looks and, taking my hand in his and entwining our fingers, he said: 'I want to meet your family and I want you to meet mine. What's the chance of my folks and yours spending Christmas together? It'd have to be at your place because my parents' house only has four bedrooms. Don't you think that would be great? And there's something I particularly want to ask your Dad.'

He looked as excited as I felt, so I didn't think it through. A vision of both our families singing carols, curled up in front of a roaring log fire, popped into my head. The perfectly shaped Christmas tree in the sitting room laden with baubles and twinkling lights and a mound of presents waiting to be opened huddled beneath, added to the scene. The whiter-than-white snowflakes falling softly onto a previous layer of crisp, crystalline snow, topped the whole thing off. I'd said yes before I'd even considered asking my family if they had other plans.

I knew they wouldn't, of course. My family always spends Christmas at The Hall and it never occurred to me that that would ever change. I also knew they would welcome Art's family with open arms. What I didn't know was that those arms would be empty due to a serious lack of cash.

They didn't really have much choice but to agree. Art insisted we Skype both sets of families to tell them the good news and because of his mum's job, we told his family first. He wasn't sure of her TV schedule and if she couldn't fit it in, we'd have to split Christmas between the families.

Art's mum, I should explain, is none other than the celebrity host and star baker of *Cornish Cooking with Camilla Camlan-Brown*. I hadn't actually seen the show until I moved in with Art, but now we watch it every week and I have to say, I've learnt a great deal about cooking that I didn't know before. Not all of it good – although I haven't said that to Art, obviously.

I suggested once to Merrion and Bella that they might like to watch it. Merrion called me the following day to tell me what she thought.

'Thanks for that,' she said. 'That's an hour of my life I'll never get back. I think they should rename it, *Hubble, Bubble, Toil and Trouble*. The woman looks like a witch and the only ingredient I recognised was the bacteria in her very obviously Botoxed forehead.'

Bella was less scathing. 'The show must be popular or they wouldn't still be screening it after three years. It was... interesting and definitely entertaining but there wasn't a lot of cooking in the episode we watched, and I had no idea pineapples came from Cornwall.'

I agree there do seem to be a few… inaccuracies in the show and the make-up department could possibly rethink Camilla's 'look', but the show goes out to a world-wide audience and Camilla receives lorry loads of fan mail every week. Art says that only a tiny minority of it is hate mail and death threats, so she's clearly exceptionally popular.

I look at my list and decide I need a glass of wine. Or possibly, one of Aunt Vicki's Christmas Cocktails. If I'm considering drinking a glass of green, bubbling and smoking liquid, I'm obviously not thinking clearly, so I defer all alcoholic beverages for the time being and make a new list. I know I should probably simply call it a day and go to bed, as I've been up for over twenty-four hours, but I've been told that the way to beat jetlag is to adjust to local time as quickly as possible, so I'm determined to stay awake for at least a few hours more.

This time I decide that only the main rooms downstairs and the bedrooms which will be occupied by the Camlan-Browns should be on the list. I'll ask Bella to lock all the doors to the other rooms and pretend they're being cleaned or something. I suppose I could always say they're occupied by loony relatives, but as I want to make a good impression, that's probably not my best idea. I could pretend chest-loads of the family treasure are kept in them, but that would sound as if we don't trust the Camlan-Browns with the silver, so again, that's a non-starter. Perhaps I should simply tell the truth and say that there's a distinct possibility that anyone entering one of them, risks either falling through the floor, or a ceiling landing on their head.

I think I'll say the rooms are being redecorated. Telling the Camlan-Browns that a life-threatening accident awaits behind each door may give them doubts as to the safety of the rest of the place and the 'closed for cleaning' option sounds as though my family live in squalor, but as I make a note of that, I realise I need to add another thing to my list.

The windows throughout The Hall look like they haven't been cleaned for months. They may be large for the most part, but little enough light shines through them during the short days of winter when they're clean. It'll seem as if we live in a land of never-ending night if the layers of dirt aren't removed.

It must be around four p.m. because I'm in the Long Gallery and the arched windows are turning a greyish shade of orange as the setting sun tries to find a chink in the grime. I've watched many a sunset from the cushioned window seats and antique chairs. They're positioned in front of the row of windows so that you can either study the family portraits of past generations or, more interestingly, take in the astonishing views. From here, you can see all the way down the long drive towards the village, on a clear day. In summer, the village is hidden by the trees but in winter the bare branches of several of them allow you to spy the stumpy tower of the Norman church and the rooftops and chimneys of many houses over which the sun sets low in an opalescent sky.

Merrion joins me and I see she's holding two glasses in one hand and a bottle of champagne in the other. I wonder just how many bottles of the stuff she is able to fit into her designer bag.

'I stocked up the last time I was home,' she says, as if reading my mind. 'I thought you might need this. How's the list coming?'

'Like one of Reece's experiments, it's a work in progress. And it's just as likely to blow up in my face. I've realised one thing though. One or two areas have drastically deteriorated over the last two years but the rest of the place hasn't changed much at all.'

'Well, that's a good thing then... isn't it?'

A long, melancholic sigh escapes me. 'No. It simply means that I'd become so used to stepping over rotting floorboards and dodging falling clumps of ceiling plaster that I hadn't realised how bad it really all is. What on earth will Art and his family think?'

I drop onto the seat of a red velvet covered armchair and I swear the whole thing shakes beneath me as if it'll break in two at any moment, so I move to the window seat and even that creaks and groans. I know Ralph said I've put on weight but I'm still a UK size 12 so I can't be that heavy.

Merrion pours the champagne, hands me a glass and sits in one of the other chairs, which I'm irrationally pleased to note, creaks just as loudly when she sits down.

'They always sound like that,' she says. 'But look on the positive side. If the chairs all break, at least we'll have plenty of firewood.' She raises her glass in a toast. 'Welcome home, Harri. Here's to a very Merry Christmas.'

As we own several acres of woodland, firewood is about the only thing we're *not* short of but I manage a smile and raise my glass to hers.

'To a very Merry Christmas,' I say. 'And hopefully, to a miracle or two in the meantime.'

Chapter Nine

I decide I should call Art. The sooner he and his parents know that The Hall isn't quite the resplendent stately home they may be expecting, the better. I'll jokingly say it's more like a bit of a ramshackle state of what such a home should be. Merrion's gone off to get another bottle, so I curl up on the window seat and press the icon of Art's gorgeous, smiling face on my phone contacts list.

'Who the hell is this?' Art snarls, when he eventually answers my call.

'It's me,' I say, disappointed that he doesn't recognise my sultry tones. 'It's Harri.'

'Jeez, Harri. Don't you know what time it is?'

'Yes. It's about five-thirty. I meant to call you earlier, sorry, but you won't believe what's been happening here.'

I can hear him sucking in a long, slow breath. He usually only does that when he's annoyed and doesn't want to lose his temper.

'It's four-thirty, Harri.'

I glance at my watch, feeling a teensy-weensy bit tipsy. 'No. It's definitely five-thirty.'

'In the UK, yes. But here in Aus, it's four-thirty in the morning and as much as I would love to hear your news, now isn't the time. I'll call you later. Bye.'

'But, darling, I want to…' I'm talking to a disconnected line and as I check my watch once more, I remember that I set it to UK time during lunch. I also remember there's an eleven-hour time difference between Hall's Cross, UK and Sydney, Australia. 'Oops,' I say out loud, before mimicking Art in a jokey sort of way. "Oh, Harri, darling, it's so good to hear your voice. I love you. I miss you. I can't wait to see you again and hold you in my arms. Oh, Harri." I make stupid little kissing sounds into my silent phone and it's only then I realise someone's standing in the doorway; and it isn't Merrion back with another bottle. It's Lance.

I give a little cough and shove my phone into the pocket of my jeans, wondering why he's in the Long Gallery.

'Merrion sent me,' he says, and it's obvious he's trying very hard to suppress a bout of hysterical laughter. 'I've brought pizza. In case Bella hadn't been able to get the oven working.'

I know Bella hasn't because Merrion told me when she brought the champagne that things weren't looking promising on the roast potatoes front, although there was a possibility we might be having boiled chicken and mash.

Quite why Lance is here though is beyond me. Was he going to be joining us for our evening meal? Just how friendly with my family is this man?

I force a smile but as I walk towards him, he watches me. When I reach the door, he steps back just enough to let me pass. I'm only inches from him and can smell the subtle hint of the sandalwood aftershave he's wearing.

'Was that your boyfriend on the phone?'

I look into his eyes, feeling like a startled gazelle coming face to face with an exceptionally powerful and extremely male, lion.

'It's impolite to listen to other people's telephone calls,' I say, dragging my eyes from his face and edging past him, breathing in as I do so to avoid any part of me touching any part of him.

'Even if they're clearly talking to themselves?'

I can hear the amusement in his voice and I spin round and glare at him.

'Especially when they're talking to themselves. Why are you here, anyway?'

He tips his head a fraction to one side. 'I told you. I've brought pizza.'

'Why didn't Reece, or Merrion or Ralph, come to get me? Why you?'

He furrows his brows. 'Does it matter?'

I continue to glower.

He shrugs. 'They were all doing other things. I put the pizza boxes on the kitchen worktop and as I was nearest to the door, Bella asked if I'd mind nipping up to tell you supper had arrived. Merrion told me you were here, so here I am. Why do you call yourself Harri?'

I'm thrown by the sudden change of tack.

'Er. Because it's my name. It's short for Harriet.'

'No, it isn't. It's short for Harold. And another name for Henry – but I've never understood why.'

He seems to be considering the matter and I see that as my opportunity to get away. I march ahead but glance back at him and as haughtily as I can I say: 'All my family and friends call me Harri. And it's Harri with an 'i' not Harry with a 'y'. But you can call me Harriet.'

Feeling rather pleased with myself I sashay towards the stairs. Unfortunately, I catch the heel of my boot in the frays from the rug, and trip. I manage to grab the balustrade and steady myself and I'm sure he hasn't noticed.

'You okay?' he says, from a mere inch or so behind me.

I don't know how he got there so quickly and it irritates me that he's pretending to be concerned.

'I'm fine. I caught my heel on the rug, that's all.'

I march down the stairs, gripping the banister as tightly as I can.

'Oh. I thought it was because you and Merrion emptied an entire bottle of champagne this afternoon,' he says, with that now so familiar tinkle of merriment in his deep and annoyingly sexy voice. 'And not all your family call you Harri. Vicki calls you Harriet and Reece and the twins call you Hairy. I think I know which I prefer.'

I ignore him and walk faster, each oak tread creaking as I trot down the stairs.

'The tread third from the bottom is loose on this side,' he says, coming down the stairs behind me. 'Mind how you go there... Hairy.'

I hope the carved Grecian Urn atop the newel post at the foot of the stairs is also loose. I'm going to pick it up and hit him with it if he says another word.

Chapter Ten

Lance won't take a penny for the pizzas – which is probably just as well because other than Merrion and possibly Aunt Vicki, none of us has got one to spare.

'You're providing the wine and wonderful company. I'm providing the pizzas. I think you're the ones getting the worst end of this particular deal.'

I'm tempted to agree with him but I won't be that facetious. We're sitting in the dining room gathered round the Tudor oak refectory table, and like the chairs upstairs, virtually each one of these chairs creaks. There's a roaring log fire in the massive hearth and to my surprise, a scruffy-looking little black dog is curled up fast asleep on the worn, Persian rug in front of it.

'Where did that dog come from?' I can't make out the breed and it looks like a mixture of several.

'He came with the pizza,' Lance fires back, that annoying little twitch tugging at his mouth.

Merrion grins. 'What? A DOGOF instead of a BOGOF?'

'Don't be ridiculous,' I say. 'You wouldn't get a second dog free if you bought one dog. That doesn't even make sense.'

'Many things in life don't make sense,' Dad says, patting my hand.

'Like love.' Ralph looks wistful.

'Ooh, Ralphie,' Merrion teases, nudging him in the ribs. 'You got the hots for someone?'

Ralph blushes. I don't think I've ever seen Ralph blush. Perhaps Merrion is right.

'Anyone we know?' I nudge him too as I'm sitting to his other side.

'Judging by the amount of time he spends in The Cross in Hand,' Aunt Vicki states, 'I assume it's the barmaid.'

Ralph turns crimson, and it's not from the heat of the fire because we're sitting opposite it, and most of the heat is blocked by Lance, Aunt Vicki and Reece.

'The dog belongs to Lance,' Reece informs me, succinctly changing the subject. 'His name is Thunder and Lance and his sister found him abandoned one night during a storm.'

'You've got a sister?' I sound like a cross between a banshee and a four-year-old and everyone gives me an odd sort of look. Even my own four-year-old brothers. Everyone that is, except Lance.

'I've got two. One five years older. One fifteen years younger.' He looks across at Dad who's sitting at the head of the table. 'By the way, Wyndham. I met that guy in the pub. The one I mentioned earlier, who knew someone who's got some roof tiles going spare. I spoke to the other guy this afternoon and I'll pick the tiles up tomorrow. And Bella, there's also a virtually brand new cooker they don't want.' He glances at Bella and smiles.

'That's very sweet of you Lance, but we can't afford it,' Bella says.

'It won't cost you a thing. The tiles are free and the man's wife has decided she doesn't like the cooker, but it's been used once or twice and there's nothing wrong with it so the store won't take it back. It so happens that the man wants some detailed advice regarding an extension. I've agreed to share my expertise in exchange for the cooker – and the tiles. I can get it and the tiles here tomorrow in one of my trucks and get one of my guys to fit the cooker.'

'That's so generous of you, Lance,' Dad says. 'But we really can't keep taking advantage of you like this.'

I can see from the look in her eyes that Bella would love to accept Lance's offer, but before she says a word, Aunt Vicki thumps her wine glass on the table and airs her views on the subject.

'Stuff and nonsense. If the man wants to give us a cooker, we should take it and be grateful. If you think I'm going to live on soup, or boiled food or pizza for the rest of my life, you've got another think coming.'

'I'm sure we can find a way to repay him, darling,' Bella pleads with Dad.

Dad knows when he's beaten. 'Well, if you're sure, Lance. Thank you so much. If there's anything of ours you fancy in exchange, I'll gladly come to some arrangement.'

Lance darts a look in my direction and from the expression on his face and the light in his dark eyes, for a nanosecond I actually think he's going to ask for a quick romp with me! I can't stop the look of horror rushing across my face and he winks at me before turning his attention to Merrion.

'Actually, I think there is,' he says so slowly that the words simply ooze sex and his eyes fix on Merrion as if he can't wait to get his hands on her.

Even she looks a little anxious. At least I think it's anxiety. I can only see her profile and Ralph is in my way, although she does seem to be grinning at Lance in what I can only describe as a decidedly coquettish fashion, so I may be wrong.

'Oh yeah,' she says, leaning forwards. 'And what might that be?'

She's sitting directly opposite him and there's a definite hint of frisson in the air, but it seems I'm the only one who feels it because everyone else carries on eating and drinking as if Lance is about to ask Merrion for one of the chillies on her pizza.

He takes a slug of wine and grins at her. 'Let me borrow your new Audi for the day on Tuesday. I need to go Christmas shopping and mine's in for its service that day. I don't want to drive around in one of those awful courtesy cars. And if you'll also come with me and give me the benefit of your shopping expertise, I'll throw in some new pots and pans to go with the cooker. I know someone who can get them at rock-bottom prices.'

'Deal!' Merrion says, beaming at him. 'I'll even do the driving.'

Lance shakes his head and looks serious. 'No, Merrion. I'll be doing the driving. That part of the deal is non-negotiable.'

Chapter Eleven

I toss and turn all night in spite of the fact I'm exhausted. I haven't slept since Saturday and that was on the plane coming here. I shouldn't have had that champagne with Merrion. Or the wine with supper. Or the chillies on the pizza. And I definitely shouldn't have eaten all of Ralph's chillies, too.

Perhaps it's the wind keeping me awake, and I don't mean the indigestion variety. I mean the positively Arctic wind that's rattling not only all the windows but also every door. It's racing down the corridors just as Merrion said, and it's not just whistling, it's bellowing as loudly as it can.

I'd forgotten about the sounds such an old house makes... until tonight. The creaks, the whispers, the rattling and banging and I hope the footsteps I heard on the floor above me, just after midnight, were those of a member of my family taking a late night stroll. But there's no guarantee they were made by the living; the dead move as freely in houses like this. Or so Aunt Vicki's always told us. She believes in stuff like that.

She's lived in The Hall for her entire life. Her brother was Dad's father and Aunt Vicki never married. She was engaged once, but her fiancé went off and got himself killed in the Second World War. He'd left his beloved dog with her and the poor thing died three weeks later. She's hated men and dogs ever since... until Lance, that is, and that curled up bundle of black fur that was sleeping on the Persian rug during supper. What was its name? Oh yes. Thunder.

What a strange name to call such a little dog. And for a man like Lance to give it. But then he does drink green cocktails, and would be perfectly happy to have a son who blows things up, so I suppose I shouldn't really be surprised. To be honest, I'm not sure anything would surprise me about that man. Although the fact that he's got sisters did, for some reason that doesn't quite make sense to me.

He seems to know an awful lot of people who know someone who's got something useful to my family. And that's a little odd too, now I come to think about it. Not that I want to think about it. Lance is of no interest to me. I'm in love with Art.

I may as well get up. There are things I could be doing instead of lying here awake. My mind is in turmoil and I really wish I hadn't agreed to Art's family coming to spend Christmas. I can't stop thinking about what a complete disaster it may turn out to be. I've seen photos of his parents' house in

Cornwall and it's not only in pristine condition on the outside; it's so clean and sparkling inside, with white walls, woodwork, rugs and accessories, and shiny black leather sofas, that it actually hurt my eyes to look at it. It's a complete contrast to The Hall.

When Art finally returned my call at ten p.m. last night, just as Lance was leaving, I did tell him he might want to mention to his family that The Hall is in the early stages of a complete refurbishment. It wasn't a total lie. I've made a list of all the things requiring attention and a list must count as one of the early stages, mustn't it?

It was nine a.m. on Monday in Sydney when he called. He told me he was running late because he'd overslept, so he couldn't talk for long. I asked him if he'd had a bad night and all he did was tut, so he was obviously in a rush. But before he rang off he did add: 'Yeah. And thanks so much for calling me.' Aw. He clearly misses me as much as I am missing him. At least I think that's what he meant.

Perhaps that's why I can't sleep. Art's not in this bed with me. I hug one of the pillows and snuggle up, closing my eyes and imagining it's him, but when I see black hair, dark eyes and lips that twitch at the corner, I shove the pillow away and decide it's time to get up. Art's hair is blond, his eyes are blue and his lips never twitch. With Art you either get a full-on smile, a frown, or nothing. There's no in-between with him. You know exactly where you stand with Arthur Camlan-Brown. He wouldn't flirt with your stepsister after giving you the eye. He wouldn't make fun of you simply because he can. He wouldn't...

What on earth am I doing? Am I actually comparing Art to Lance? I need coffee and I need it now. And perhaps I should take a paracetamol or two. I'm obviously suffering from far more than merely jetlag.

Chapter Twelve

'Good gracious, darling, you're up early.' Bella pours me a large mug of milky coffee without asking if I want one. She knows me so well.

'Couldn't sleep,' I reply, yawning my head off before going up to her and kissing her on her cheek. 'Good morning. Why are you up before the crack of dawn?'

'I couldn't sleep either.' She gives me a quick hug before handing me the coffee and the open biscuit tin, which is full of her homemade shortbread.

I take the coffee and three shortbread triangles and perch on a chair near one of the windows. There are three large windows in this kitchen; two face the front lawn and drive, and one overlooks the kitchen garden to the side, with its winding path leading to the apple orchard and onward to the woods.

I stare past the rows of polytunnels eerily illuminated by the lights from the kitchen, into the total darkness beyond. After waking up to the bright lights of Sydney each morning for the last two years it's both calming and unsettling at the same time. A draught creeps in through the closed window and I can hear bare branches sway and the leaves of the evergreens rustle faintly in the distance. That's where the holly and the pine cones are; apart from one or two holly bushes and pine trees planted here and there either side of the drive, most of them are in those woods.

'What time did Lance say he and his band of merry men would be arriving with the cooker?' I ask, biting into the soft, crumbling texture of a golden-baked triangle.

'He's picking it up at eight, so allowing for loading that and the tiles, he thinks he'll be here by nine.'

'What does he do, exactly? For a living, I mean. Is it all kinds of building work, or does he specialise? Does he have his own business? He said one of his men will fit the cooker so I assume that means he must, and that he has a team of some sort. Where does he live and where did he come from? And why does he seem to spend half his time at The Hall?'

Bella raises finely arched brows. 'My word, darling. That's an awful lot of questions for this early in the day.'

'Well, he seems rather friendly with the family and he walks around The Hall as if the place is his second home and yet I know nothing about him.'

'That's because you live so far away.'

'I don't see how that makes a difference. We all speak every few days. Why has no one ever mentioned him?'

She looks at me askance as she kneads a mound of dough which I know will shortly transform into heavenly-smelling, freshly baked bread.

'I'm sure we have, darling. You make it sound as if we've been keeping him a secret from you, and why on earth would we want to do that?'

'That's what I'd like to know. And he's not the only secret you've been keeping. No one told me what was going on with Dad or that Ralph was set upon or that Reece blew up the kitchen and scullery for that matter. Why wasn't I told any of this?'

Bella frowns, abandons the dough and hugs her coffee mug to her chest. 'I suppose we have kept one or two things from you, darling – but only for your own good. There was hardly any point in us telling you about the financial situation, or about the incident with Ralph because you would have been worrying yourself sick over it all and what could you do? You live thousands of miles away. I assumed Reece would've told you about the kitchen and I know Ralph mentioned Lance to you only the other day. He told us you wanted Lance to do some titivating to The Hall in time for the Camlan-Browns' arrival.'

I feel a little offended. Or perhaps I just feel left out. I get the fact that none of them wanted me to worry and I also realise I couldn't do much from the other side of the world, but that's not the point.

We've always been such a close family and we tell each other everything. Well, almost everything. We do keep one or two things back, I'll be the first to admit that. But it really feels as if I've been kept in the dark about so many things and I can't help having just a tiny bit of a sulk about it.

'Okay. I can understand you not wanting to tell me stuff that might worry me. We discussed that last night. But why hasn't anyone told me that Aunt Vicki has suddenly decided she likes men and dogs, for instance? Or are you saying I would have been worried about that, too?'

Bella grins. 'We must've told you about that. Although perhaps in the beginning, we were a little worried. It was such a sudden transformation that your father and I wondered if dear Vicki might be suffering from rapid onset dementia or something equally as horrid.' She shakes her head. 'Did we honestly not tell you about the effect Lance and his gorgeous little dog has brought about?'

'No, Bella. You didn't. And when Ralph mentioned Lance the other day, it was the first time I'd heard about the man.'

She looks genuinely surprised. 'I can't think why. The dear man's here almost every day.'

'That's precisely my point!'

I'm getting just a tiny bit cross. Since I came home I've been told several times by several people – including Lance – that I live so far away. It's almost as if, because I'm thousands of miles away I'm no longer included in the minutiae of everyday life at The Hall. As if it no longer concerns or affects me. But it does concern me. And it hurts to feel… left out. When I wished Aunt Vicki 'pleasant dreams' last night she looked at me with tearful eyes and said: "So much has changed since you went away, child, but it was your choice to go and you're building a new life for yourself." I know this is ridiculous but I'm not sure I want a new life if it means losing my old one. Why can't things be like they used to be? Why can't I still be included in life at The Hall? It is just as much my home as it is everyone else's. At least, to me it is.

Bella comes to me, sits on the chair beside me and gives me a great big hug.

'I'm so, so sorry my darling. We didn't keep anything from you on purpose. Truly we didn't. Well, we did keep the things we thought would worry you, but not the good things. Not Aunt Vicki's change of heart and certainly not Lance coming into our lives. He's been like a gift from the gods, so I honestly have no idea why none of us has ever told you all about him. The only explanation is that when we speak to you, we all want to know *your* news and what's happening in *your* life. We want to hear all about you and Art. About what you've been doing and the places you've been. We don't want to go on about what's been happening here.'

'But *I* want to know what's happening here. Whenever I've asked you've always said something like, "Oh, life's going on as usual at The Hall".'

She pulls a troubled face. 'I suppose for us, it is. Apart from the unpleasant parts.'

'And your "gift from the gods".'

'Oh yes. And Lance. But he came into our lives as a result of an unpleasant situation, so perhaps that's why we didn't mention him at first. I suppose it now feels as if he's so much a part of the family that we sort of assume you know all about him and even speak to him yourself. Which I now see is ludicrous, of course. Why would you speak to him if you didn't even know that he was here?'

Dad shuffles through the doorway in his dressing gown and slippers, the hems of his striped, brushed cotton pyjamas dragging on the floor.

'Good morning, sweetheart. Aren't you a sight for sore eyes? I didn't expect you to be up and about for a few hours yet. Is something wrong?'

He looks so pleased to see me and also somewhat concerned that I haven't got the heart to tell him how I feel.

'No, Dad. Nothing's wrong. I simply couldn't sleep. I think it's because I'm so happy to be home.'

He comes across and kisses me on the forehead.

'And we're so pleased you are. We've all missed you more than you can imagine. Are the twins still asleep?'

The question's directed to Bella of course and already I feel left out again. I really must get a grip. I'm behaving like a brat.

'Yes, thank heavens.' Bella smiles at me. 'Yesterday's excitement completely wore them out.'

'I didn't think that was possible,' Dad says.

He laughs and pinches one of my remaining biscuits but I smile up at him because that was something he always used to do. Whenever I had biscuits, or chocolate or anything, he would jokingly come and pinch some, even if he didn't go on to eat it.

'Oi! Get your own. There're plenty in the tin.'

'Ah. But yours are always so much nicer. We'll have some breakfast and then we'll get started and see if it's possible to knock this place into shape, without it falling down in the process.'

'Morning,' Merrion says, ambling into the kitchen. 'At least I think it's morning. I need coffee, Mum. And lots of it. Morning Dad. Morning Harri.'

'Morning darling. Oh! And Ralph... And Vicki... And Reece? Is that really you? My goodness. Everyone is up with the lark today.'

'The lark isn't up yet,' Aunt Vicki says. 'I'm only up because there's so much noise I can't sleep. Everyone's been thumping and crashing about. It's enough to wake the dead.'

'Morning everyone!' I say, smiling brightly as they each return my greeting. I'm so pleased, it feels as if my heart may burst out of my chest and my previous sulky mood is forgotten. It's foolish, I know but to see my family gathering in the kitchen for morning coffee and biscuits takes me right back to the day I left and I have to do everything in my power to stop myself from weeping; I'm so overcome with emotion.

'I hope it hasn't woken the terrible twins.' Merrion dashes as far away from the door as possible. 'I'm not ready for those two just yet.'

Shrieks of laughter followed by something crashing down the stairs tells us all that yes, the twins are awake. I wonder if the crashing sound was one of them falling from top to bottom but no one seems concerned, so I assume this happens often.

'We'd better find them something to occupy themselves if we're all going to be working on sprucing up The Hall,' says Dad.

'Don't look at me,' Merrion says. 'I'd rather climb a ladder and help fix the roof than handle those two.'

'So would I,' Aunt Vicki snaps, as Dad glances in her direction. 'I'm no babysitter.'

'I'll send them off to collect pine cones and build a place in which to store them,' Bella tells us. 'That should keep them busy for an hour or two.'

'Remind them to build it at ground level,' Ralph says. 'I'm not climbing up a tree again to get them down.'

Bella nods and makes more coffee and the first hint of daylight peeps over the treetops as Theo and Thor come racing into the kitchen, dragging a broken chair behind them.

'He did it!' Thor says, obviously seeing the expression on Dad's face and quickly pointing at his brother.

'You told me to! We want to make a slidy thing for when it snows really, really lots.' Theo beams, not showing the least bit of remorse as he holds up one of the chair legs. 'It broked when Thor told me to jump on it.'

Thor giggles. 'It broked some more when we tried to get it down the stairs. Is Lance here? He's gonna help us.'

Merrion tuts. 'It's '*broke*,' and Lance is '*going to*' help,' she says in an attempt to correct them.

The twins look at one another and back at her. 'We just said that.'

'I give up,' she replies, and pours herself more coffee.

'You gonna help too, Dad?' Thor asks.

'And Hairy?' Theo suggests.

Thor shakes his head. 'She's a girl. Girls don't like making stuff cos their nails get broked. Lance said so.'

'Oh he did, did he?' I need to have a word or two with Lance. 'Well, Lance is wrong. I love making things and so do lots of girls – and women. I'm a woman.'

Thor frowns deeply but Theo merely giggles and shrugs before shrieking at the top of his voice: 'It's snowing!'

They both drop the chair and rush to the front windows almost knocking Aunt Vicki over in their haste. I twist round and glance out at the kitchen garden. The twins are right. It is snowing. And it's coming down thick and fast.

Chapter Thirteen

It's only when Lance arrives a few hours later that I realise Bella didn't answer any of my questions about him. He's driving a beaten up old pick-up truck containing row upon row of roof tiles and Thunder's in the seat next to him. By now the snow must be about an inch deep and the dog looks excited. I can see from where Merrion and I are standing beneath the colonnade that his paws are on the dashboard and he's barking and wagging his tail for all he's worth. The second Lance stops and opens the door, Thunder dives headlong into a layer of snow and promptly tumbles head over heels.

'He may be exceedingly cute but he's not very bright,' I tell Merrion as we both watch his antics.

'Lance? Or Thunder?' She grins at me and gingerly makes her way down the snow-covered steps to greet them.

Dad, Ralph and Reece are already standing near where Lance has parked and are clearly planning to help unload the tiles, in spite of the weather.

'Don't tell me you've come to help?' Lance asks Merrion, as she joins them.

'I've come to supervise,' she replies, kissing him on the cheek.

I can't believe she did that, although I don't know why. I remember that last night, Bella, Merrion and even Aunt Vicki all either gave Lance a peck on the cheek, or he did so to them. Thankfully, Art called me just as Lance was leaving, so I avoided the situation by giving Lance a quick wave goodbye and dashing away to speak to Art in private.

When I carefully walk down the steps and join them, I make sure I stand well away from Lance. I have no intention of kissing him and I certainly don't want him kissing me, even if it's only a quick peck on the cheek.

'It's snowing,' I say, somewhat foolishly.

He gives me an odd look as if he can read my mind, and smiles. 'So I see. Another supervisor?'

I must admit, he does have an incredible smile. It's one of those smiles that seems to be able to force you to smile back, even if you don't want to.

'No. I'm here to help,' I reply, beaming at him.

I expect him to make some remark about this being 'man's work' or that he wouldn't want me to 'break my nails' and I'm ready with a comeback.

'They're heavier than they look. So only take a few at a time,' he says. But not to me. He's saying it to Reece who's trying to lift several at once. What he does say to me is: 'They're dirty, so I hope those are old clothes.'

They're not of course. For some reason I'm wearing my best jeans, a jumper that I know is rather flattering on me, and my leather jacket.

He grins. 'There's an old fleece of mine in a holdall in the passenger seat footwell. You can put that on if you like.'

I hesitate and he misreads me. 'It's clean,' he says, that twitch of his working overtime.

I don't particularly want to wear something belonging to him, even if it is clean, but neither do I want to ruin my clothes. While I'm still hesitating, he moves to the door and pulls out the fleece which he tosses in my direction. Now I don't really have a choice. I take off my jacket and he holds out his hand to relieve me of it.

'I'll put this on the seat,' he says, looking me up and down. 'Nice jumper.' He grins and turns away.

I can feel my face burning and I quickly put on Lance's navy fleece and hope that no one else has noticed.

'Aw look,' Ralph says. 'Harri is embarrassed. The colour suits you.'

'Thanks,' I hiss at him.

The fleece swamps me and I shove up the sleeves so that my hands are free. Lance passes me a pair of workman gloves.

'I don't need gloves,' I say, trying to prove that I'm just as capable of dealing with the cold and snow as he is.

'Suit yourself. They're there if you want them.' He brushes some of the snow from the side rim of the truck and lays the gloves over it before sliding his hands into another well-worn pair which he pulls out from his jacket pocket.

I really dislike this man.

I notice that Reece is wearing gloves and so are Ralph and Dad. Damn. I also realise my hands are freezing now that I've taken them out of my pockets.

Again, Lance reads my mind. He silently hands me the gloves and walks round to the back of the truck. Without another word, he starts unloading tiles into one of the three wheelbarrows he's also brought.

Yep. I dislike the man more than any man I've ever met in my entire life.

'Don't carry them like that,' Merrion is telling Ralph. 'You'll drop them.'

'I'll drop them on you if you don't get out of the way,' comes his reply, as I join him at the rear of the truck.

'Make yourself useful, Merrion,' Lance instructs her. 'Instead of standing in the snow, go and make some coffee, please. My men should be here at any moment and they'd love a cup almost as much as I would.'

'I'm sorry, Lance.' She actually looks apologetic. 'I'll go and make some now.'

I can feel snowflakes landing on my tongue and realise my mouth is hanging open.

Before I even know what's happening, Lance reaches out and, with the tip of one finger, lifts my chin up so that my mouth is closed.

I really, really, *really* dislike this man.

I slide an armful of tiles towards me and try to flip them to make a pile which I can lift into one of the wheelbarrows but they are *definitely* heavier than I thought. Again, without a word, Lance takes some of the tiles from me, leaving a far more manageable pile.

A large white van roars up the drive and comes to a sliding halt a few feet from Lance's truck. Three men jump out and immediately come and help, exchanging greetings with everyone as they do so.

One of them looks me up and down and grins but all he says is: 'Lovely weather, isn't it, love?' He makes no comment about the fact that I'm helping, or the way I look.

Now there are so many of us, the tiles don't take long to unload. We're putting them into the three wheelbarrows and ferrying them to the woodshed at the side of the house near the parking section. From there they'll be taken to the various places they're required, but how we're going to repair the roof without scaffolding is a mystery to me.

We stop for the coffee and biscuits (in the shape of gingerbread men) that Bella and Merrion bring out to us and we all take shelter in the woodshed – apart from Thunder, who is running around in the snow as if he's having the time of his life. That dog's as crazy as his master.

'The scaffold will be here before lunch,' Lance says, answering my unasked question. 'We'll get that up regardless of the snow, although the forecasters say it won't last and they give sunny spells for this afternoon. I've got floodlights coming at the same time so if we work through into the evening, we'll have the roof done by tonight.'

Dad looks as surprised as I am but Ralph merely nods in agreement and Reece begins calculating ways of getting the tiles up to the roof.

'There's an electric conveyor hoist coming,' Lance informs Reece, placing a hand on his shoulder. 'You could help work that for us if that's okay with you.'

'Absolutely.'

Reece beams up at Lance as if the man has bestowed a great honour on him, instead of merely utilising free labour. But as I have no idea how we're going to pay for any of this, we need as much free labour as we can get.

'I think we need a quick word, Lance,' Dad says, walking away from the relative warmth of the woodshed in the direction of the house.

Lance follows Dad and so does Ralph. I decide to do the same. We walk to the colonnade where we can still shelter a little from the snow.

'I can't afford this, Lance.' Dad doesn't mince his words. 'It's really very kind of you to organise it all and naturally, I'll pay you for your time so far but as for a scaffold and—'

Lance holds up one hand in a stop gesture. 'Wyndham, don't give it a second thought. I've got plenty of scaffolding and a lot of it's currently sitting in my yard doing nothing, so there's no cost involved in that. The men were working on another job but we're waiting for windows and sliding roof lights from Germany, so they were also sitting around doing nothing today. I'm paying them anyway, so they might as well get something done.'

'But it's still costing you money,' I point out.

Lance does a double take as if he's only just realised I'm there. I'm standing to one side of him so I suppose he probably has.

'Let me worry about that.' He looks Dad directly in the eye. 'You and your family have been good to me, Wyndham, and to Gwen. You've made us feel more at home than we have for a long time. And in any case, believe me, I won't be out of pocket.'

Gwen? Who's Gwen? Does Lance have a wife? He doesn't wear a wedding ring; I noticed that the first time I laid eyes on him. A girlfriend? Surely if he had, she would've come with him last night? Perhaps Gwen's one of his sisters. That would make more sense. Especially as he said that one of them was fifteen years his junior – which would mean she's about fifteen or so, depending on how old Lance is, exactly. I've assumed he's roughly the same age as Ralph. And me. Now he's really got my curiosity going. Does that mean his younger sister lives with him? If so, where's their mum? Or does he still live 'at home'? And why haven't they felt at home anywhere else? Are they travellers or something? Do they find it hard to settle in one place for long? And just *how* has my family been 'good' to him and to this... Gwen? I know my family would welcome anyone with open arms but that sounded as if they have gone above and beyond.

Dad is shaking his head. 'You've repaid us tenfold with everything you've already done for us. Especially dealing with all that unpleasant business and assisting me and Ralph. We can't continue to take advantage of your kindness and generosity, Lance.'

Lance sighs, long and deep. 'You're not taking advantage of anything other than friendship, Wyndham. Friendship which is given with no strings attached and no expectations. It's Christmas. Can't a friend do something for his friends without being made to feel guilty about it?'

Ralph pipes up: 'Lance is right, Dad. We shouldn't be giving him a hard time about wanting to help. I'm sure we'll be able to return the favour one day. Until then, let's get on. It's bloody cold standing around here.'

Dad looks slightly relieved and when Lance taps him on the arm in a friendly gesture, he turns to head back to the woodshed.

'Lance,' I say. 'May I ask you something personal, please? You and Ralph go ahead, Dad. We'll be with you in just a second.'

They all exchange glances but Dad and Ralph walk on and Lance comes back and stands directly in front of me, only inches away. Which frankly, there's no need for. Neither of us is blind or deaf.

'How personal?' He seems apprehensive.

I peer around his broad shoulders to check that Dad and Ralph are out of earshot.

'Oh, it's not personal at all. At least, not like that. Although I would like to know more about you because at present I know absolutely zilch. But we'll save that for another time. But... who's Gwen?'

He grins and I have to say that he looks rather smug. 'Gwen's my younger sister. She lives with me... for the time being. And no, I'm not married and I don't have a girlfriend. But how is that not personal?'

I give a little cough. 'That's not what I wanted to talk about. I just wondered, that's all. And for the record, I wasn't asking about your love life. I'm not in the least bit interested in that.'

His grin widens and his eyes twinkle with merriment. 'What *did* you want to ask me?'

'It's about the... titivating I'd like done – as you and Ralph keep calling it – and which I shall insist on paying for. I've made a list.'

He tuts. 'Don't you start. I'll do whatever you want me to and it won't cost you a thing – apart from the actual cost of Christmas decorations because those, I don't have. Paint, yes, Christmas sparkle, no. Although I do know someone who may be able to get some stunning decorations at a rock-bottom price. We'll talk about it tomorrow night.

And if you insist on paying for something, you can buy me dinner.'

'But… you're going Christmas shopping with Merrion tomorrow.' Which is a stupid thing to say, given the circumstances. What I should have said was: 'No.'

'During the day, yes. But we'll be back in plenty of time for dinner. Oh good. Here come my men with the cooker. I'll book the restaurant so leave that with me. I'll pick you up at eight.'

'What?'

He's already down the steps and halfway towards the second white van to arrive at The Hall today.

I really, really, *really* dislike that man.

And now I'm wondering what to wear tomorrow night.

Chapter Fourteen

I don't get a chance to speak to Lance for the rest of the day and if I didn't know better I'd think he is trying to avoid me. I simply don't understand the man. Why does he want to discuss my list over dinner? I know it's not a date or anything – but dinner? Really?

I must stop obsessing over this. Dinner is as good a time as any to discuss business. It's no different than a working lunch. I've had lots of those with male colleagues and friends and never worried about it. So why have I spent all day thinking about dinner with Lance?

When I checked and cleaned all the dining room silver, I wondered if I should mention it to Art. Sorting the table linen, bed linen and towels, I tried to recall exactly what was said. I even attempted to discuss it with Merrion but all she said was: 'What's the big deal? It's Lance. And he won't make you pay, I'm pretty sure about that.' Which of course was missing the point entirely. And actually made matters worse.

I took out tea and biscuits to the men this afternoon in the hope of catching Lance. The forecasters were right. The snow stopped by lunchtime – which the men all worked through – and just before twilight, the sun showed its face. Lance was up on the scaffold, his own face bathed in sunshine, and he wouldn't come down. Not even for tea. And certainly not for me, although I did ask him.

'Can it wait?' he said, before clambering higher.

So why am I now sitting at one of the kitchen front windows, watching Lance beneath the floodlights throwing snowballs for his mad dog, Thunder to chase, all the while wondering what I should wear tomorrow night?

'They've almost finished patching up the roof,' Bella says, breaking into my thoughts. 'I can't believe that for the first time in months we may have a roof which doesn't leak.'

'I can't believe it's not going to cost us anything.'

Bella gives me a questioning look. 'That sounds as if you think it might. As if you don't... trust Lance, or something.'

I shrug and move away from the window. 'I don't know him. I only met him yesterday. There's something about him that worries me but I can't quite put my finger on it.'

'Nonsense.' Bella's tone is sharper than she intended, I'm sure. 'Lance has a heart of gold, and I'm sorry darling, but you really should get to know someone before you start casting aspersions on their character.' She turns away. 'I'm making tea. Would you like a cup?'

That certainly told me.

Before I have a chance to reply, Reece strolls in, reaches for a glass jug and starts mixing his green goo.

Bella smiles at him. 'Before I forget, Reece darling, the new cooker is strictly out of bounds. Is that perfectly clear?'

Reece nods. 'That reminds me. Aunt Vicki wants to know what's for dinner. Now that we have a working oven once again.'

'Roast chicken. The one we were going to have yesterday.'

'That's my favourite.'

Well, at least Reece is happy. I wait until he takes his concoction to our aunt before I go to Bella and give her a hug.

'I didn't mean to upset you. You're right. I don't know Lance. I won't say another bad word about him until I do. And he certainly has been exceptionally generous. We're going out for dinner together tomorrow night, so that should give me the ideal opportunity.'

'Oh?' Bella doesn't seem quite as pleased as I thought she would be. 'Are you sure that's wise?'

'Wise? It's not a date, Bella. I wanted to discuss the list of things I'd like him to do to prepare The Hall for Christmas. He didn't have time today and he's going Christmas shopping with Merrion tomorrow, so discussing it over dinner makes perfect sense. We've both got to eat.'

'You can both eat here.' She pours me a cup of tea, and slides a plate of mince pies dusted with icing sugar, towards me. 'They're still warm. I thought I should test the new oven before I put the chicken in.'

They look delicious and I tell her so. I take a bite of one and the syrupy mincemeat makes my taste buds dance.

'I can taste cranberries. And zesty orange. Wow! Definitely brandy. Cherries. And are those pecan nuts?'

Finally she smiles at me. 'Yes. I hope they're still your favourites.'

'They are. And so are you.' I hug her again. 'I'll make dinner tonight. You really should sit down and rest. You've been on your feet for most of the day and you need to take care of yourself and my soon-to-be, brother or sister.'

She hugs me back before rubbing her tummy. 'It's strange, you know. At this stage, with the twins, they were kicking and moving constantly. This little one hardly moves at all. If Andrew, our doctor, hadn't been quite so certain, I might think he had made a mistake.' Her head shoots up and panic fills her eyes. 'You don't think there's something wrong, do you?'

'No,' I say, rather too quickly. 'No of course there's nothing wrong. It's probably a good sign. I mean, Theo and Thor haven't stopped moving since the day they were born, so they simply did the same when you were carrying them. This little one will clearly be calm, quiet and a total joy to behold.'

'I'm sure you're right.' She smiles and takes my hand. 'I'm sorry I snapped at you.'

I smile back and squeeze her hand in mine. 'You can snap at me anytime you like. You're pregnant. You can blame your hormones.'

'Now that, my darling, is a very good idea. I can blame my hormones for everything from here on in. What a delight that's going to be.'

Chapter Fifteen

'Where is everyone?' I ask Aunt Vicki, opening the door to the sitting room and walking towards her to check that she's awake. And still alive. The woman sleeps like the dead.

It's almost six o'clock and dinner's in the oven, so it seems the perfect time to get on with something else. I remembered, when I was peeling the potatoes, that I hadn't been through our Christmas decorations to see which we could, or could not use. They are stored in the attic rooms and there are boxes and boxes of them. I want someone to come with me but no one seems to be around.

Aunt Vicki shakes her head. 'No one tells me anything, so I don't know why you're asking me. But it just so happens that Merrion did mention taking Pegasus for a ride and Reece is cleaning the stables and grooming Sirius while she's gone. The twins, allegedly, are helping. Wyndham popped down to the village with the list Bella gave him for the Christmas cake ingredients, and Ralph ran off after him because of several things Bella forgot. And Bella, I believe, is having a leisurely soak in the bath. Apart from that, I've no idea.

As that covers the entire household, it seems the only person available to venture into the attic rooms with me is Aunt Vicki and I know before I ask her, that won't be happening.

'But it's dark out. Why would Merrion ride Pegasus in the dark?'

Pegasus is our horse, and Sirius is our donkey, although as I've already mentioned, sometimes it's difficult to tell which is which. Pegasus isn't white, and definitely doesn't fly, unlike his namesake. He's the same colour as Sirius: a sort of grey-ish brown, and Aunt Vicki could outrun him. Sirius, unlike *his* namesake, is absolutely *not* the brightest star in the universe. Nevertheless, we love them both.

Aunt Vicki tuts. 'Because that girl is determined to kill herself one way or another. But if you look you'll see there's a full moon, and that, together with all those floodlights means it's so bright out there it looks like day.'

'I suppose I'll have to leave it then.'

'Leave what?'

'I was going to sort through the Christmas decorations. Merrion's going shopping tomorrow with Lance and I thought she might see some new ones to buy while she's out. I don't want to waste money though, so I was hoping to see what we've got that still works and doesn't look as if it's older than The Hall.'

'Are there so many that you need help to go through them? The Hall's not the size of a Palace and we only decorate down here.'

'It's not the amount of boxes that concerns me. It's where they are. After hearing those footsteps last night, which no one will own up to, there's no way I'm going into those attic rooms alone.'

'Bah! A few ghosts won't hurt you any more than will the spiders.'

'Thanks. I'd forgotten about the spiders. The last time I was up there some of those were the size of a small planet.'

'Just the man we need.' Aunt Vicki is smiling past me towards the front doors. 'Lance! Lance! Come in here please.'

'No, Aunt! Don't bother him. He's been here all day. It's time he went home.'

Needless to say, she ignores me.

'Lance! Lance! Ah. You did hear me calling. I thought you'd gone deaf judging by the time it's taken for you to join us.'

'My apologies. I'll walk faster next time.' The broad grin belies the tone of sarcasm.

'Good. Now I know you've had a long day but Harriet is scared of ghosts and spiders.' She shakes her head and rolls her eyes.

I want the ground to open up and swallow me – which bearing in mind the state of this place, is actually more than feasible. Unfortunately, the floorboards hold up and I turn to see Lance chuckling. Yes. The man is chuckling.

'That's very interesting,' he says. 'I don't particularly like sharks.'

Aunt Vicki frowns. 'There are no sharks in our attics.'

'And now we've repaired the roof, there's no rain water either. Or snow.' He's clearly trying not to burst out laughing, although I'm not sure what's funny about that.

'Thanks,' I say, hoping to change the subject. 'You must be exhausted. Let me show you out. I'm sure you can't wait to get home and put your feet up.'

'I'm not exhausted. Today was just an average day. But I was just about to go home and I only popped in to say goodnight.'

'Good night then.'

'I'm in no rush. If you need me to catch a spider, I've got time. I expect all the work on the roof has disturbed some. I'm not sure how to remove a ghost though but I'll give it a try.'

'That's very kind. But I'm fine.'

Aunt Vicki pipes up. 'No, you're not. You said you want someone to go into the attic rooms with you. Take Lance. He'll be far better protection than Merrion. Or Ralph.'

'I don't need protection. I... I just wanted someone to help me carry the boxes down, that's all. It can wait.'

'Lead the way,' Lance says, stepping aside, with a smile. 'Thunder's fast asleep on the passenger seat of my truck so I'll leave him where he is. I think he tired himself out today and he's curled up on my fleece you were wearing. He seems to like your perfume.'

'Harriet! Don't just stand there. The man has better things to do than spend his evening watching you dithering.'

There's not much I can say or do. I've now got to go into the attic rooms with Lance. And for some peculiar reason, that frightens me more than ghosts or spiders. At least I think it's fear I'm feeling. What else could the goosebumps and tingling be?

Chapter Sixteen

'My boyfriend's not afraid of sharks. And there're lots of sharks in Australia. In the water, I mean. Not actually *in* Australia.'

I'm marching up the stairs as quickly as I can and babbling away like a lunatic. I've already told him that I'm not really afraid of ghosts and that I don't believe in them. He does, apparently. I've also said that I'm not afraid of spiders – only the very big ones. He told me they are far more afraid of me – and that he feels the same. Did that mean he's also afraid of very big spiders? Or was he being rude and suggesting he's afraid of me? What a bloody cheek!

'Your boyfriend sounds like a brave man.'

I turn and glower at him. 'Are you being sarcastic?'

He raises his eyebrows. 'No.'

I continue upwards. 'He is brave. He's also gorgeous. Intelligent. Considerate. And kind. Oh. And very, very sexy.'

'He sounds perfect. How long have you been together?'

'Two years. Two wonderfully happy years.'

'That's... wonderful.'

'It is. I know my family will love him as much as I do when they meet him.'

'They haven't met him?'

'Not in the flesh. They've met via Skype and Facetime and they think he's absolutely great. Which he is.'

'I have no doubt.'

We reach the landing and head towards the stairs leading up to the attics. They're on the other side of the Long Gallery so we have to walk the entire length of that. It seems much longer when you're walking in silence and can't think of anything to say.

'Look at that moon,' he says, stopping suddenly.

I thought the dappled light shining in through the grimy windows at the very end of the Long Gallery was from Lance's floodlights; but it's not. The ones on this part of the house are turned off. Lance goes to one of the windows and wipes a large area with the sleeve of his jacket.

Moonbeams dance across the floor; shadows and dust come together in the half-light, just like women in long silver dresses waltzing in the night.

'I could look at that for ever,' I say, joining him. 'It's so beautiful. Like a platinum brooch on a black velvet dress... only much, much bigger.'

That sounded dumb even to me but when I meet his eyes, he's not laughing. Or chuckling. He's not even smiling. He's simply looking down at me. Not staring; merely looking. And it's as if his eyes have harnessed the moon's gravity and I'm being pulled closer. And closer. And—

'We'd better get on,' he says, clearing his throat as he turns away from the window – and from me.

I'm not completely sure if what I think just happened, actually *did* happen. Did I really edge closer to him? Did I really tilt my head back and look deep into his eyes? Did I really move in as if I thought we were going to kiss? Did I?

Oh my God!

No. It's not possible. It's not. It's really, really *not*.

But I know in my heart that it is.

Bugger!

I really, really, really don't like this man.

And now it's very clear that he doesn't like me, either.

Chapter Seventeen

I toss and turn for the second night running, but this time I can't blame the wind, or unexplained footsteps. The night is still and there's not the slightest breeze. There's not even a draught creeping in through the windows, and the house, for once, sleeps peacefully. Perhaps the repairs to the roof have helped stop more than the rain coming in. Is this what they mean when they sing *Silent Night?*

Maybe it's too quiet. Could that be the problem?

No. Tonight's lack of sleep is due to me not being able to forget what happened – and what didn't happen – in the Long Gallery with Lance. And now also because the tune to that damn Christmas carol seems to be on repeat play at the forefront of my mind.

I still can't believe I behaved the way I did. When Art called me earlier, shortly after I'd eaten dinner with my family, but long after Lance had left, I felt as if I'd betrayed him. He told me he was missing me and I know I'm missing him. That's the only explanation for what I did. But it's a bit of a pathetic one. The romance of the moment simply got to me. The moonlight. The darkness. The man.

I need my boyfriend; I need to have sex. And it's only been three days. No, four days. I was too busy packing on the night I left.

I've got to get some sleep or I'll look like death warmed up when Art arrives. He won't want to have sex with me if I've got bags under my eyes, wrinkles and a sallow, drawn complexion.

Perhaps I should simply get up and finish going through the boxes Lance and I carried down... in virtual silence, I might add. And not just in silence. I couldn't look at him and I'm sure he didn't look at me. He also suddenly seemed to be in a dreadful hurry to leave. When we took the boxes into the sitting room and Aunt Vicki offered us a glass of her Christmas Cocktail, Lance declined.

'Thunder may be wondering where I am,' he said. 'I'd better go. Goodnight.'

And he was gone.

Aunt Vicki screwed up her eyes and stared at me as she filled two glasses with the bubbling green goo and handed one to me. 'Did something happen in the attic?'

'What do you mean?' I croaked, before knocking back the entire contents of my glass.

'Hmm. Whatever it was it certainly scared him. I know it wasn't spiders and I'm sure it wasn't a ghost.'

'I'd better check on the chicken,' was all I could think of to say – and I even struggled to say that. I definitely won't be having another of those Christmas Cocktails. The stuff may not be poisonous but the taste is downright toxic.

Thankfully, Aunt Vicki didn't pursue the matter further.

Chapter Eighteen

The sun may be shining, the sky may be blue, but frankly I'm ready for bed.

I got up at two and trawled through the remaining boxes and it was just as well I did. By the time Merrion came down for breakfast at eight o'clock I had written a list and checked it far more than twice, and whichever way I looked at it, we will be needing a substantial amount of new decorations.

I tried to shorten the list by going through it again with Merrion and Bella, over scrambled egg on toast, followed by several rounds of toast and marmalade and copious amounts of coffee. Merrion says I also consumed two chocolate muffins and a banana, but I don't remember doing so. Anyway, none of it helped. If anything, the list grew longer.

During the last two years, it seems Merrion has become a great deal fonder of bling and sparkle than she used to be. And jewel-covered princess has always been her party piece, ever since I've known her, and long before, according to Bella, so now we are talking serious, eye-popping, iris-burning, lighting displays and decorations. Which I have to admit is fine with me. Apart from the cost element. But Lance did say he knew someone and might be able to get decorations at rock-bottom prices. We're going to have to take him up on that. I just hope he can get them in time. Merrion doesn't seem to think it's a problem.

In spite of telling myself I won't, I watch Lance walk up the stone steps and ring the bell. It's one of those door bells that plays a selection of tunes. It's usually set to 'plain chimes', but now Ralph has set it to play 'Christmas music'. I think the battery must be flat or something, because it's not a tune I recognise.

I hover in the kitchen doorway, trying to decide whether to go back into the kitchen or run and hide, as Dad pulls the big brass knob to open one of the double doors, but it won't budge. Lance pushes it from the other side, and as it swings open, it nearly knocks Dad flying. Fortunately he manages to steady himself.

'Sorry, Wyndham.' Lance looks genuinely concerned. 'I didn't mean to push that hard.'

Dad laughs and shakes his head. 'You don't know your own strength, but it's not a problem. I'm a little unsteady on my feet this morning. We all sat up until late last night drinking sherry and eggnog. Oh... and Vicki's Christmas Cocktail.'

Oh yeah. I'd forgotten about how much we had to drink last night. Perhaps *that's* why I couldn't sleep. Although isn't alcohol supposed to make you tired?

I realise it's too late to hide, so I dash back into the kitchen and hope Lance didn't see me.

'Good morning Harriet.' His tone seems a little cooler to me.

'Morning,' I chirp merrily, without looking back but pretending a carefree attitude I'm definitely not feeling. 'Lovely day for shopping.'

'You're welcome to come with us, but I don't think there's much room in the back.'

He knows damn well there isn't; he spent some time looking over Merrion's new car, inside and out the day we arrived. It's a sports car built for two.

'That's very kind, thanks. But I've got a busy day already planned.'

He and Dad join the rest of us in the kitchen and Aunt Vicki beckons Lance to her side. I pray she's not going to ask him what happened in the attic. Although nothing *did* happen in the attic, so perhaps he'll tell her that if she asks.

'Harriet's been up all night sorting through those boxes. She couldn't sleep, apparently.'

Why is it that my family constantly feel it's okay to embarrass me? She gives me an accusatory look, as if I've been rifling through her knicker draw instead of box after box of Christmas decorations. Lance doesn't even glance in my direction.

'I didn't sleep that well myself,' Lance says, kissing her on the cheek. 'Must be something in the air.'

He still doesn't look at me but that's probably a good thing. Morning is definitely not my best time of day, and minus even the tiniest flick of mascara, or swipe of lipstick, I can say without fear of contradiction, I'm not looking my most glamorous. Unlike Merrion, who looks as if she has stepped from the pages of a magazine – and she isn't wearing any make-up either. Life can be so unfair sometimes.

'Something in the air.' Aunt Vicki repeats Lance's last sentence. 'Something in the attic, more like.'

I'm exceptionally grateful that remark appears to go right over his head. Unless he's pretending not to understand her meaning.

'It was very dusty up there,' he replies. 'No spiders or ghosts though.'

Aunt Vicki tuts. 'Harriet's made a list of the Christmas decorations we would like. I believe you said you may be able to lay your hands on some. Harriet. Give Lance the list.'

'I've given it Merrion.'

Merrion smiles and waves the handwritten list in the air. 'It's a very long list,' she tells him. 'We want lights everywhere. And we do mean everywhere. Round the pillars of the colonnade. Running along the gutters. Wrapped around the trees. We'd like rows of lights around each window, and you know how many windows we've got. We want to be able to see The Hall from the village, once the lights are all switched on.'

Lance raises one eyebrow. Just one. 'With that many lights, you'll be able to see it from the moon. Um. There is one minor point I should mention. I'm not sure your wiring is up to coping with all of that. Especially as we haven't yet replaced the old fuse box at the rear of the house.'

'Who cares about the rear of the house?' Merrion says, frowning. 'No one looks at the rear.'

Ralph, who until now had been remarkably quiet, seems to feel this is a good time to add to the conversation.

'Let's hope no one looks at Harri's rear. Not after she's eaten such a huge breakfast.'

'I think what Lance means, Merrion,' I hastily suggest, ignoring that remark, 'is not that there'll be lights at the back of The Hall, but that the old fuse box, which happens to be situated at the back, isn't up to coping with that many lights at the front.'

'That's precisely what I meant,' Lance confirms. Yet he still doesn't look in my direction.

Dad rubs his chin with his thumb and forefinger. 'Didn't we have the fuse box replaced a few years ago, Ralph?'

Ralph nods in agreement, and so does Lance, before adding: 'But that new consumer unit only connects the new wiring for the main front rooms. They didn't rewire the entire house and they left the old fuse box intact. I'll see what I can do.'

'Don't tell me,' I say, without thinking. 'You know someone who knows someone who happens to do rewiring at a rock-bottom price.'

That didn't come out quite the way I meant it to but finally, Lance looks at me, though there isn't any laughter in his eyes, and his mouth doesn't twitch at the corner.

'No. I can do the rewiring myself. We should go, Merrion. If you're ready.'

'Ready, willing and able.' She beams at him and gets up from her chair. 'See you all later. Have fun. And Reece. Try not to blow anything up while we're gone.'

Lance gives a perfunctory wave and says a quick goodbye and as Merrion links her arm through his, they head towards the front door.

Bella gives me an odd look. Something between concern and reproach. 'That sounded a little ungrateful, darling, although I'm sure you didn't mean it to.'

Dad nods in agreement. 'Lance didn't seem his usual self this morning. I hope everything's okay.'

'I meant it as a joke,' I say.

'You can explain that to him later,' Dad says, smiling reassuringly.

It's only when I hear the car roar down the drive that I realise Lance didn't mention dinner. Now I don't know if our evening's on or off and even if I had his phone number – which I don't – I can hardly call or text him after what I've just said and the way he reacted. Or what I did last night. Because every time I go over it, I know it was me who moved towards him. And he was the one who turned away.

Have I mentioned how much I dislike that man? Now I dislike myself almost as much.

Chapter Nineteen

Today feels like a very long day. My eyes are burning, my head is spinning, and my body longs for sleep – even though it's not yet six-thirty. But I know there's no point in going to bed because, as tired as I am, my mind simply will not stop racing.

I don't know why I'm making such a big deal about this. People do stupid things all the time. As long as no one gets hurt or dies, what does it matter? There are worse things in life than making a complete and utter fool of yourself.

At least I've kept myself busy. Lance may not have been here today but to my surprise, his men have. The ceiling in the Queen's Room has been repaired, repainted and re-plastered where necessary and Ralph and I have cleaned all the windows, both in that room and everywhere else besides. The men have kindly said they'll clean the outsides before the scaffolding comes down. They've also said they'll hang the lights once Lance gets them. Which they seem pretty certain he will.

The kitchen smells heavenly and the aroma of spices, fruits and brandy has been wafting around The Hall for the most part of today. Bella has been baking sausage rolls, mince pies, meringues and pastry cases, and we finished making the Christmas cake and extra Christmas puddings about fifteen minutes ago. The mixture is still in the bowls so that Merrion can have a stir and make a wish when she returns from shopping. Even Aunt Vicki helped. Although she did drink quite a lot of the brandy as she added it to the various mixes. "One for the bowl, one for me," seemed to be her saying of the day.

I've poured Ralph and me a glass of wine and am about to sit down when Merrion returns. Her face flushed, her eyes bright and she's smiling from ear to ear.

'What a day! Pour me one of those please.' She flops onto a chair and lets out an exaggerated sigh.

'I take it you've had a good time,' Bella says, smiling at her clearly exhausted daughter.

Merrion nods. 'Even better than I expected. I knew I'd have fun with Lance but gosh, I'm so tired. I think I'll go and take a bath.'

'We've saved the cake and pudding mix for you to make your wish,' I tell her.

She beams at me. 'Thanks.' She jumps up and rushes to the bowls. Stirring each one in turn, she closes her eyes and obviously, makes her wish. 'Right. I'm going upstairs. Will someone please call me when it's time for dinner?' She kisses us all on the cheek and dashes towards the door. She stops and glances back at me. 'Speaking of dinner. Lance asked me to remind you, Harri, he's picking you up at eight.'

'Oi!' Ralph shouts, as I choke and my wine spurts out all over him.

Chapter Twenty

As Merrion didn't return until six-thirty, it's already ten-to-seven by the time I climb into the bath. I know it would be quicker to take a shower, but they don't always work terribly well at The Hall and besides, I need to lie down and close my eyes for five minutes at least. I can do that in the bath.

Merrion has given me some divinely scented bath oil and as I luxuriate in the warm water and skin-softening perfumes, I nearly fall asleep. As much as I would love to stay here I don't have time for this. I have no idea what I'm going to wear and I have to dry my hair and put on some make-up. I keep telling myself it's not a date. I've got a boyfriend and I love him very much, but I still want to look my best. Even though there's not much chance of that. My eyes are red and puffy and a five-minute catnap isn't going to cure that.

I drag myself from the bath, wrap a fluffy white towel around me, and see Merrion sitting on my bed.

She smiles at me. 'I thought you might like to wear this.' She runs her fingers over a simple but beautifully cut and undeniably elegant, red dress, which is lying beside her on the bed. 'Don't worry. It'll fit. A friend of mine is a designer and I asked him to make you a couple of gorgeous dresses for Christmas. This is one of them. Its skirt is made from viscose and virgin wool, and the bodice is velvet. You can't have the other dress until Christmas Eve.'

I can feel a huge lump in my throat as my eyes well up. 'Oh Merrion! It's stunning.' I run my hand over the baby-soft velvet bodice with its wide, V-neckline and little capped sleeves, and down the length of the A-line skirt, which I know before I even try it on, will flatter my figure.

'Put it on,' she says. 'Then I'll do your hair and make-up.'

I hesitate for just a second. 'This isn't a date, Merrion. And the dress is incredible, but we're probably only going to the village pub.'

She frowns. 'I know it's not a date. But it's Christmas. Every woman should look stunning at Christmas no matter who she's with or where she's going. And he's not taking you to the pub. He's taking you to *Ophelia's Garden*, and believe me that place is posh. I've been there. It's his sister's restaurant.'

'His younger sister owns a restaurant?' That was something I didn't expect.

Merrion laughs. 'No. Not the younger one. She's called Gwen. The restaurant belongs to Ophelia, Lance's older sister. She's a chef.'

I didn't expect that, either.

'Hurry up,' she says. 'We don't have long and we've got to dry your hair before I can do it up.'

I slip on my undies and step into the dress. It just so happens that I've brought a pair of high heel, red suede, ankle-strap shoes with me which will match perfectly. I sit at the dressing table and close my eyes while Merrion transforms me from a pale, puffy-eyed drab-looking woman, into a peaches and cream, clear-eyed, stunner – even if I do say so myself. With my long hair piled into a loose bun, with wispy curling tendrils, and a pair of Merrion's diamond earrings, I'm almost unrecognisable.

As I walk into the kitchen behind Merrion, Ralph wolf-whistles and even Reece says: 'Gosh, Hairy. You look rather good.' Which for a nerdy fifteen-year-old is equivalent to saying he thinks I look bloody amazing.

Bella clearly isn't sure what to think. 'You look beautiful, darling. Perhaps a little too beautiful. I hope Lance doesn't get ideas.'

I laugh. 'There's no chance of that. I don't think I'm his type.'

'You're every man's type, looking like that,' Aunt Vicki tells me, and I think it's meant to be a compliment.

'You look just like your darling mother,' Dad says. I can see a mixture of pride, sadness and love in his eyes.

'I think that's Lance,' says Merrion, as a strange-sounding Christmas tune plays, like a music box winding down.

I walk towards the door and feel as if I'm a teenager going to her prom. Dad comes with me and pulls on the doorknob as Lance shoves the door from the other side, a little more gently this time. My family gather in the kitchen doorway, including Aunt Vicki but as the door swings slowly open, they dive out of sight, and even Dad walks away, waving his hand in the air in a greeting to Lance.

'The dress was a present from Merrion,' I say, as his eyes travel up and down the length of me.

'That's some present,' he replies. 'You look… completely different. And yet… the same.'

I have absolutely no idea what that's supposed to mean.

'Er. Thanks. I think. You look… different too.'

He does. He looks drop-dead, bloody gorgeous. And clean-shaven. His suit, although casual, is clearly expensive and I recognise a designer-label, white shirt when I see one. Merrion's shown me several photos of male models over the years, and tonight, Lance could be one.

I throw on my leather jacket, and Lance offers me his arm.

'The steps are a bit icy in places. The snow may have melted and the sun's shone all day but the temperature has definitely dropped tonight.'

That surprises me. I'm feeling rather warm.

'I hear you had a good day with Merrion.'

He smiles at me for the first time since yesterday. 'I did. I hear you had a busy one. I spoke to one of my men this evening.'

I'm surprised to see we're walking towards a chauffeur who holds open the door of a sleek looking limo.

'I know someone, who knows someone who runs a limo business.'

My eyes meet his and I'm glad to see that he's still smiling.

'I think I should apologise for what I said this morning. It didn't come out the way I meant it.'

'Apology accepted,' he says, as I get in. He walks round to the other side and slides in beside me. 'I thought we'd go for fish and chips.'

I know what Merrion said, but I'm not completely sure he's joking.

'Great. As long as there's mushy peas and I can have three pickled onions, that's absolutely fine with me.'

He bursts out laughing and it feels as if a great weight has been lifted from me.

I love my boyfriend, Art. I know I do. But it seems I may not dislike Lance quite as much as I hoped I would.

Not that it really matters. Lance made it clear last night that he's not in the least bit interested in me. And anyway, it seems pretty obvious that he's rather keen on Merrion. I can't help but wonder where all of this is heading. One thing is for certain, Merrion was right. I don't think this Christmas is going to turn out quite the way I expected.

Chapter Twenty-One

The limo pulls up outside the door of *Ophelia's Garden*. The restaurant sits in the grounds of a privately owned estate and was once, so Lance tells me, a cattle shed.

Inside, it's a haven of understated wealth and glamour. I recognise several people from the television and sporting worlds seated at the bar.

A stunning, dark-haired woman walks towards us, smiling.

'I'd like you to meet my sister,' Lance says. 'But she's not here. This is Libby, her restaurant manager and friend.'

'I'm pleased to meet you, Harriet, and good evening, Lance. Let me show you to your table.'

'I'm pleased to meet you too,' I say, a little surprised she knows my name. But then I suppose even Lance may have to book ahead.

We follow her to a table which sits on a raised dais, in front of a large, curved window. It overlooks a floodlit waterfall about eight feet high and which cascades into a similarly lit fish pond below. The water is surrounded by rocks, and plants and flowers of all shapes and sizes tumble over them from top to bottom. From this table, we have a view of virtually the entire restaurant, and yet, thanks to discreet and tasteful Japanese-like screens, the restaurant clientele can't really see us.

Libby hands Lance a green, leather-bound wine list and I assume, like several men I know, he'll believe it's his God-given duty to choose the wine we're going to drink. I feel I should dissuade him of that notion just for the hell of it when he says:

'What's your favourite wine?'

'Oh. Um. Anything in a glass.' Emmeline Pankhurst would be so proud.

He smiles. 'We'll have the usual, Libby.'

I glance at my menu and see that mine does not have prices. In these days of equality, I can't help but smile.

'I think I have the wrong menu,' I say. 'I'm paying for dinner.'

He grins and we swap menus, but this one doesn't have prices either.

'If one needs to ask the price, one shouldn't be eating here.'

The words trip off his tongue but the comment doesn't suit him. Libby returns before I have a chance to reply, and I can't help feeling just a touch of panic as I see she's bringing champagne. What with that and Lance's comment about the prices, I may have to sell several body parts to pay for this.

'But you're not paying,' he says, 'and please don't argue.'

I don't. I can't afford to. I wait until Libby has poured the champagne and left us.

'So where is your sister?' I ask. 'You said she's not here. Did you mean this evening? Or that she's away on holiday or something?'

'She's in Aspen, Colorado with her husband and kids. They have a second home there and they'll be staying for a month. My other sister, Gwen, is with them.'

'Wow. Your sister married someone rich.'

'No. Her husband did. The money belongs to my sister. Although she doesn't tell many people that.'

This man is full of surprises.

'Merrion told me your sister is a chef.'

He smiles and nods. 'A very good chef. But you probably won't have heard of her. Ophelia doesn't like fame or all that celebrity nonsense.'

'So... how did she make her money? Or did she win the lottery or something?'

'Something,' he says, and takes a drink from his glass. 'I think I've sorted out the Christmas lights and decorations. I'll hopefully get them before the end of the week. I'll do some work on the wiring and we'll have them up by the weekend. When's your boyfriend and his family arriving? I'm sure Merrion said something about Mrs Camlan-Brown's TV schedule. Does she work in front of, or behind the cameras?'

'I see we've switched the conversation from your sister to my boyfriend's family. I assume that means you'd prefer not to answer any more questions concerning your nearest and dearest. Perhaps the same goes for me.'

He shrugs. 'Let's talk about something else then. Have you decided what you'd like to eat?'

'Yes,' I say, paraphrasing from my menu. 'I'll have the fish and chips with mushy peas.'

He throws back his head and laughs. 'And the champagne jus?'

'Naturally. What's fish and chips with mushy peas without the champagne jus? It's nothing short of blasphemy.'

Chapter Twenty-Two

The evening passes far too quickly and when it comes to an end, I'm a little disappointed. The food was delicious and I'll never be able to eat fish, chips and mushy peas again without remembering this night. Of course my meal, when it arrived piping hot and presented like something an art gallery would be proud of, looked nothing like the fish, chips and mushy peas I've ever had. It tasted nothing like it either. An offering of paradise on a plate wouldn't be an over-exaggeration.

I'm not surprised that Lance isn't required to pay. If my sister owned a restaurant and had a second home in Aspen I wouldn't expect to pay either, but I am surprised that he leaves Libby and the staff a substantial tip.

The limo is waiting right outside, the engine ticking over as the chauffeur holds the door. And then we've pulled up outside The Hall before I know it and Lance is walking me to the door.

The night sky is a black canopy of stars and the moon is my spotlight as I take centre stage but I'm not sure how to act. For an evening that wasn't a date, this has been the best first date I've ever had.

Lance, I've discovered is older than Ralph and me by three years. Unsurprisingly, he loves fast cars and loose women. Although I think that second part was said tongue in cheek. He does like women though and despite the fact that he refused to discuss his love life – by adeptly skirting around my questions or simply changing the subject – I'm pretty certain he's no monk. He did talk about Merrion each time I mentioned her, but I realised it's more in the way that Ralph does: like a sister or a friend rather than a love-interest.

On the topic of love-interests, he also refused to confirm or deny the rumours of Ralph and one of the barmaids from the village pub. "Ask Ralph," is all he'd say.

He'd definitely like kids one day but if they don't happen naturally, he will happily adopt.

'Unless I happen to find one abandoned, like my dog, Thunder,' he joked. Whose name was given to him by Gwen, not by Lance.

And marriage. On that subject he seemed rather vague. 'Who knows what life has in store?' That was the end of that discussion.

We reach the front door and I smile up at him but I make sure I'm standing a few feet away. I wouldn't want a repeat performance of last night. The moon is just as full and I'm definitely longing for romance – and not just romance, if you get my drift. Best not to take any chances.

'Thank you for a wonderful evening,' I say.

'Thank you,' he replies. 'Perhaps we can do it again one day. Although as your boyfriend arrives next week and there's still so much to do, I don't suppose we'll get the chance.'

Um. Shouldn't that have been my line?

'That's a pity,' I reply. 'Oh. Not that Art's arriving next week. I didn't mean that. I meant it's a pity we can't do this again.'

'I know,' he says.

His eyes fix on mine and time passes us by. Out there in the world monumental things are happening. People are dying; people are being born. And everyday things. People are setting off for work; some are coming home. And life-changing things. Couples are fighting and going their separate ways; others are coming together and falling in love.

I have a wonderful, yet at the same time, awful feeling that Lance and I are in that final group. At least, I'm pretty sure I am. I'm not quite as sure about him.

Damn it. I really, really, really *like* this man.

Merrion is absolutely right. This Christmas is definitely not going to turn out the way I expected.

So much for us all having a very Merry Christmas. I wouldn't be surprised if it all blows up in my face.

And that's without any help from Reece.

Chapter Twenty-Three

I can't believe it. I slept like the proverbial log. I thought I'd toss and turn all night, riddled with guilt. Torn by emotion. Thrilled with excitement remembering the look in Lance's eyes when we finally said goodnight. And that was all we did. *Say* goodnight. He didn't even give me a peck on the cheek like he does with the rest of my family. I turned my key. He shoved the door open and with a final look at me and the briefest smile, he left without another word, pulling the door firmly closed between us.

And yet this morning, I feel like a new person. The sun is shining, there isn't a cloud in the sky and I firmly believe The Hall *will* be transformed from a dilapidated pile into a fairy-tale castle in plenty of time for Christmas. Well, not quite a castle. Although with Lance and his men on the job, even that's a possibility. I'm sure Lance knows someone who knows someone who could lay their hands on a couple of turrets, the odd round tower or two, and a handful of battlements. With Lance, anything seems possible.

I shower, dress and run downstairs for breakfast.

'Good night?' Ralph asks, grinning at me over the rim of a Christmas-themed mug.

I smile back. 'Yes, thank you. You?'

'Fabulous.' There's a note of sarcasm in his tone. 'Merrion, Reece and I nailed back loose floorboards, filled several holes and washed down all the skirting boards. I can't remember the last time I had so much fun.'

'Aw, thanks, Ralph.' I go over to him and give him a great big hug. 'Where are Merrion and Reece? And where are Bella and Dad?'

'They're all outside with Lance.'

'Lance? He's here early.'

Ralph shakes his head. 'You're up late. It's almost nine o'clock.'

At the precise moment I glance at my watch, Merrion comes bouncing in from the Great Hall. And I do mean, bouncing. She's got her booted feet on some sort of pogo stick-like contraption.

'My watch has stopped,' I say, before asking Merrion what, exactly, she is doing.

'Isn't it wonderful?' She beams at me and Ralph. 'Reece adapted it from Mum's old pogo stick. It bounces much higher now. We can use it to help us hang decorations and stuff that's out of reach.'

'Or we could simply use a ladder,' I suggest.

'Spoilsport.' Merrion stops bouncing and jumps down to the floor. 'So how was last night? I was going to wait up, but I thought it might cramp your style.' She grabs a mug and pours herself coffee, grinning all the while.

'You seem to be forgetting that I have a boyfriend.'

She shakes her head and pulls a face, the grin now plastered right across it. 'I wasn't the one out on a date.'

'Nor was I. It wasn't a date. We simply discussed… Christmas. And everything that needs to be done beforehand. And before you ask,' I add hastily as I can hear Dad and Bella approaching. 'Nothing happened. He didn't sweep me into his arms and kiss me passionately. He didn't even give me a peck on the cheek.' I see both Merrion and Ralph shoot a glance towards the door and I turn my head only to wish I hadn't.

Lance is standing just inside the doorway, with Bella and Dad some way behind, and it's clear from the expression on Lance's face that he definitely heard at least the last part of my comment, if not all of it.

'Coffee?' Merrion quickly asks. 'And let's have some of those delicious Christmas cookies Mum baked yesterday.

Dad and Bella walk past Lance. 'Coffee sounds wonderful. It's freezing out there. I wouldn't be surprised if it snows again.'

'I hope it does,' Bella says. 'Although it would be preferable if it could wait until next week. Or better still, until after the Camlan-Browns arrive. We don't want bad weather to delay their journey, or even worse, to mean they have to cancel. That would be so disappointing for you, wouldn't it, Harri darling?'

Lance and I have been staring at one another for the entire time, and it's only when Bella hugs me, that I drag my eyes from his.

'Sorry, what? Oh yes, of course. Very disappointing.'

I can hardly say that the way I'm feeling right now, the Camlan-Browns cancelling would probably be a blessing in disguise.

Chapter Twenty-Four

Yet again, Lance seems to be avoiding me. After the little 'fiasco' in the kitchen this morning, he took his coffee and a Christmas cookie outside, simply saying that he "had better get on". I was considering following him and trying to talk things through, but Dad got there first.

'I'll join you,' Dad said.

Merrion gave me one of her looks; this time the one that left me in no doubt that she thinks I'm a lost cause.

'What happened to grabbing opportunities when they arise and worrying about the consequences later?' She frowned at me and shook her head.

Bella looked at Merrion and across at me. 'Opportunities? What opportunities?'

'Nothing important,' I said. 'I'd better go and see what else needs to be done.' I took my coffee and two Christmas cookies and headed outside.

'Opportunities might not be there forever,' Merrion called after me. 'You should give that some thought.'

'I will,' I said.

And I've done nothing but think about it ever since. The problem is though, this thing with Lance, whatever it may be, may not be an opportunity at all. He's looked at me once or twice in a way that's made my heart race faster than Merrion's car, my breath come in shorter gasps than Aunt Vicki's when she's on her way upstairs, and my head spin quicker than the cement mixer I'm currently standing beside. But other than that, he hasn't actually *said* anything to indicate that he's interested in me. And he definitely hasn't *done* anything to make me think he is. Quite the opposite, in fact. Each time I think something might happen between us, he turns and walks away.

Merrion is right though. Since my mum, and her dad, passed away, we've all lived by the phrase, carpe diem: seize the day. We've all believed in grabbing opportunities while we can and worrying about the consequences later, as Merrion said. But this time I'm not sure that's the way to go.

By telling Lance how I feel, I risk making him uncomfortable if he doesn't feel the same. His friendship with my family is equally as important to them as it is to him and I can't, and won't, do anything to jeopardise that. I'd hate him to avoid coming to The Hall because of me.

But if he does return my feelings, what then?

My boyfriend and his family will arrive next week, and Art, I'm sure, is planning to propose. We've been together for around two years, and I know I love him. At least I did, until I met Lance. Now I'm not so sure. If you love someone, can you want to kiss someone else? To be in someone else's arms? Yes, I suppose you can. But surely not if you *really* love them. And that's what I'm not sure about. I don't think I *really* love Art. Not enough to spend the rest of my life with him, in any event.

So what should I do? Should I call and tell him? Should I cancel our Christmas get-together? Should I suggest we take a break? Or should I just leave things as they are and see how this all plays out? Perhaps sometimes it's wise to take some time. To go with the flow and see where it takes you.

I think that's what I'll do. This Christmas may not turn out as I expect, but one way or another, I'm convinced it's going to change my life.

Chapter Twenty-Five

It's been four days since I went on my 'non-date' with Lance. Today is Saturday, and Art, together with his parents and his sister, Morgana, arrive this coming Friday, the day before Christmas Eve. To say that I'm panicking is a massive understatement. Apart from the roof, The Hall looks worse from the outside than it did when I arrived last week. Lance and his men have been chipping off plaster and pulling out bricks like Reece chips off the icing and picks out the raisins in Bella's delicious iced, fruit muffins. Dad keeps telling me that sometimes things have to get worse before they get better, and I'm hoping he's right.

I can't help feeling that statement also applies to my love life. Lance has hardly spoken to me since that business in the kitchen, the morning after our dinner, and does everything in his power to ensure we're never alone.

Art on the other hand, remains blissfully unaware of my turbulent emotions and each time we speak he reiterates how excited he is at the thought of meeting Dad and being able to ask 'his question'. He still won't tell me what it is, but I'm sure there's only one thing it can be. I mean, what else could he possibly want to speak to my dad about apart from that he wants to marry me?

I've been trying to drop a few hints that marriage may not be something I want to rush into. I told him I'd been reading about divorce rates, and that I'm surprised anyone wants to get married these days.

He laughed. 'Haven't you got anything better to do than read that rubbish? I thought you wanted to go home early to spend time with your family and get The Hall ready for our arrival.'

I don't have the heart to tell him that I don't think The Hall will ever be ready for their arrival, and it doesn't seem right to tell him over the phone or via Skype or FaceTime that I'm having serious doubts about our relationship. I definitely can't tell him by phone that I think I may have inadvertently fallen in love with someone else.

At least I think I have.

I'm fairly sure I have.

So life goes on as normal. Except nothing any of us are doing is 'normal' at the moment.

Ralph is currently replacing missing putty in several of the windows; Merrion is washing and re-hanging curtains; Bella is cooking and freezing festive fayre as if we may be hit by a stray comet at any moment and will need enough food and drink for at least a year. She's even persuaded Aunt Vicki to help and with several jugs of that Christmas Cocktail close at hand, Aunt Vicki is definitely getting into the Christmas spirit. Both inside and out.

Dad is somewhere assisting Lance, which basically means that neither of them are within looking or speaking distance of me. Lance is making sure of that. Reece is trying very hard not to blow things up, but of course, he's failing at that. We've lost one bath, two cupboards, one wardrobe, and there's now a bare patch and a hole in the front lawn, which was never there before, and which actually *does* look as if we've been hit by a comet. A comet named Reece.

And me. I'm watching paint dry. Literally. The paint I've just slapped on the walls in the Opal Room needs to dry before I can rehang the paintings and photos that were scattered on the walls. It's a bit of a last-minute job. The Queen's Room, where Art's parents will be sleeping looks as good as it's ever likely to and so does the Lilac Room, amazingly, in which Morgana will stay. But, having decided that it might be wise to have an additional, habitable bedroom available in case things go rapidly downhill between me and Art, I've chosen this room as the one in which he can stay. Rather conveniently, it's the furthest room from mine and although it is habitable, it needs some serious redecoration.

I'm still sort of hoping the room will not be needed. At least not by Art. That this is merely a strange phase I'm going through, and the moment I see him and he wraps me in his arms, I'll realise it is Art I want to be with.

And not some utterly inscrutable builder I only met seven days ago.

Theo and Thor burst into the room – and Thor steps right in the middle of the paint tray which is sitting on the floor. He obviously realises he's done something which may upset me because he instantly steps back out and points to his brother.

'Oops. Theo pushed me.'

'Didn't!' Theo yells, giving Thor an almighty shove.

Thor stumbles backwards and lands on his bottom. For a second I think he may burst into tears but his eyes open wide and so does his mouth. He points his finger at the footprints he's made in *Egyptian Sand* Vinyl Matt and a grin as wide as the Nile slowly runs across his face.

I can tell immediately what he's thinking but I'm simply not quick enough. He's on his feet and, grabbing his brother by the hand, within seconds they're both jumping up and down in the tray. They're small, but two boys against a plastic tray will only have one outcome and just as I get there from the other side of the room, the tray splits in two. Thick and creamy *Egyptian Sand* sprays out like a storm and splatter's all three of us with paint.

I shriek in horror; they shriek with laughter and before I know what's happening, I hear the patter of sticky-soled boots clumping down the hallway towards the stairs.

Trying to avoid the puddles of paint, I run after them.

'Stop,' I yell. Which of course, makes them run faster.

I hear the thump, thump, thump of small feet trotting down the stairs and realise they are heading to the Great Hall. Not that I need to guess. I can simply follow their footprints.

'Stop right now,' I scream at the top of my lungs. 'Or you'll go on Santa's naughty list and you won't get any presents.'

I hear them roaring with laughter, which is a strange reaction to such a threat but as I turn the corner and reach the top stair, I can see the reason for their hilarity. Lance is at the foot of the stairs and has picked them up and thrown them each across his shoulders. He looks at the footprints and then up at me and I can see he's struggling not to laugh.

'I see you've been painting,' he says. 'Is there much on the walls? Or are the three of you wearing most of it?'

'This isn't funny.' Paint drips from my hair and plops onto the stair.

Lance bites his bottom lip and shakes his head. 'Of course it's not. It's not at all funny.' He rolls the twins down his arms, with his hand wrapped around theirs, and dangles them both in the air like a hunter with his catch. 'What do you want me to do with these two?'

'I know what I'd like to do with them, but I don't want to spend Christmas in prison.'

Lance grins. 'I'll take them to Merrion in the utility room. She can get them cleaned up.'

'She *will* be pleased.' I walk down the stairs towards him carefully avoiding the paint-footprints. 'You are definitely going on Santa's naughty list,' I tell the boys.

Thor giggles. 'We're on it already. Mummy put us on.'

'So did Daddy,' Theo adds.

'And Merrion,' Thor says, proudly. 'And Auntie V put us on in November.'

I can see Lance shaking with suppressed laughter.

He glances back at me and grins. 'You and your family need to find a new threat. At this rate there won't be room for anyone else on Santa's naughty list.'

'Don't encourage them,' I snap, finally catching up with him and marching past. 'Excuse me. I need to see if Merrion has something to remove this paint from my hair.'

'If she doesn't, come and find me. I can dunk you in a bucket of turps. That should do the trick.'

I turn my head and glower at him. 'Thank you. I shall certainly bear that very kind offer in mind. I'm so glad that if nothing else, at least I provide you with amusement.' I shove the utility door open and

Merrion bursts out laughing, which doesn't help my self-righteous indignation one little bit.

Lance follows me in, and deposits the twins in the large stainless steel sink.

'I'll leave them to you, Merrion,' he says, no longer grinning.

With a final look at me, he walks back out, apparently not in the least bit bothered that his clothes are covered in paint. But then I suppose they are his working clothes, and they're already coated with many building materials other than paint, so it doesn't really matter.

Chapter Twenty-Six

Having scrubbed my skin to within an inch of its life and finally removed virtually all traces of *Egyptian Sand* from my hair, I pull on a pair of black trousers and a jumper Bella knitted me. It's bottle green and on the front is a huge white snowman with a smiling face, an orange knitted carrot-shaped protrusion for its nose, and beady eyes that swish to and fro every time I move. It sounds rather tacky, but I love it. I've even got fluffy, dangly snowman earrings to match.

'You've done something different with your hair, Harri,' Ralph says, the second I walk into the dining room.

'I'll do something with yours if you're not careful.'

I'm the last one in, and it's only as I go to the empty chair to sit down that I notice Lance sitting to one side of it, and Merrion sitting to the other. She grins at me and I know for certain she's planned this. What I don't know is why she keeps trying to get me and Lance together. I'm also surprised to see him. He hasn't joined us for a meal for days. And it's a Saturday. I'm surprised he doesn't have plans.

I have no other choice than to sit where Merrion wants me to, unless I drag another chair to the table. Clearly I can't do that without making it obvious, so I sit and give Lance a brief smile.

He smiles back. 'I like the jumper. And I see you didn't need my turpentine.'

'Thanks. And no, I didn't.'

'Why are you painting the Opal Room?' Aunt Vicki, who is sitting opposite, asks me.

'In case it's needed.'

'Why would it be needed? We know who is coming for Christmas.'

'She's doing it,' Ralph informs her, as loudly as he possibly can, 'in case she and her boyfriend fall out. She wants somewhere to put him that's as far away from her room as possible.'

I can feel Lance looking at me but he doesn't say a word and I daren't look round at him.

'Why would they fall out?' Aunt Vicki persists.

Ralph shrugs. 'Don't ask me.'

'Hmm.' Aunt Vicki looks me directly in the eye. 'The Australian sun not looking quite so bright now that you've seen what an English winter has to offer?' To my horror, she stares at Lance and adds: 'We need her back here. Christmas wasn't Christmas without her.'

'What can Lance do about that?' Dad asks, grinning as if it's a joke.

'That's what I want to know,' Aunt Vicki adds. 'More than we imagine, I suspect.'

'Have some more Christmas Cocktail, *Auntie*,' I say, through gritted teeth, and we glare at one another for a second or two.

'I think,' Bella says, thankfully coming to my rescue, 'that what Vicki means, is once The Hall is spruced up and looking wonderful, our darling Harri may be tempted to come home.'

Merrion leans closer to me and whispers: 'Harri may be tempted to come home, but it won't be The Hall that persuades her.'

'Well, there's a challenge for you, Lance,' Dad says. 'Harri's return to the fold is entirely in your hands.'

Sometimes I really wish my family would simply shut up.

'I'll see what I can do,' Lance replies, but he doesn't look at me when he says it.

Chapter Twenty-Seven

It's all hands to the pump today. Figuratively speaking, of course. It may be Sunday but for us it's not a day of rest. There is still so much to do that it's frightening to check my list. But I do because I have to.

Of course it doesn't help that I have to keep adding to it. Like replacing the things Reece blows up and now removing paint from the floors and furnishings of the Opal Room. At least the walls in there are dry, so the paintings and photos can be rehung.

Last night, at dinner, Lance had a brilliant suggestion for the bare patch and hole in the front lawn, courtesy of Reece. Lance thought it would be a good place to plant one of the Christmas trees. We've had a tree and sometimes two outside the front of The Hall for as long as I can remember but Lance suggested one big tree that could be decorated with lights which would stay there all year round. It's a wonderful idea and I don't know why none of us has thought of it before. It's going to be planted today and Lance is coming to help.

All the rewiring throughout The Hall has now been done, he told us last night, which means that as soon as the front façade is decorated, the lights can begin to go up. I still can't believe it'll all get done in time, but it seems to be coming together. All we need is a few more days – and a few more days is all we have.

We're just finishing breakfast when Lance arrives at nine o'clock.

'Have you heard the weather forecast?' He joins us in the kitchen and Bella pours him coffee. 'They forecast blizzards and freezing temperatures from Wednesday until Boxing Day. That means nearly a week of heavy snow and ice.'

Merrion shrieks with excitement, as do the twins and I. Bella doesn't look so sure. Ralph shivers, as if he's cold already, and Reece asks if Lance happens to have a chain saw he can borrow.

'If there's going to be a considerable amount of snow,' Reece says. 'I'd like to try my hand at building an igloo. Or possibly something larger in which I can safely conduct some experiments without fear of blowing anything up. I'll be able to cut compacted snow into blocks – if I have a chain saw.'

His eyes light up and with his glasses sliding down his nose and his hair, as usual, sticking out in all directions, he definitely looks the part of a mad scientist. I'm not sure that letting Reece loose with a chain saw is wise but no one else seems concerned.

'Absolutely,' Lance says. 'On condition that you also build a vodka ice bar inside.'

Merrion clearly likes that idea. 'Ooh! We could have our own little ice hotel. I'm sure there were some old fur rugs up in the attic rooms. I'll go up later and look.'

'Look out for spiders and ghosts,' Lance says.

He throws a look in my direction and I'm sure there's a hint of wistfulness in those dark eyes of his.

'The spiders and ghosts need to look out for Merrion,' Ralph says.

Bella glances at the windows, where the morning sunlight is streaming in and when I meet her eyes, she smiles a little sadly. 'I hate to put a dampener on things. But Art and his family won't be arriving until Friday. If the blizzards start on Wednesday…' She shrugs and shakes her head.

'Oh I see,' Dad says. 'Art and his family may not be able to get through.'

'We don't live in the Outer Hebrides,' Ralph reminds us.

'No,' Aunt Vicki snaps. 'We live in the English countryside, and that's fifty times worse.'

'Vicki is right,' Lance agrees. 'The gritting lorries probably won't clear the country lanes.'

Reece's face lights up even more. 'I can build a sleigh, and Pegasus and Sirius can pull it.'

Merrion laughs. 'And we can stick a flashing red nose on Thunder and he can light the way.'

'No one is sticking a flashing red nose on my dog,' says Lance, but he's grinning. 'We'll need to crack on with the work to the front of The Hall though. We can work in snow and we can work in rain, but working in a blizzard is definitely a no-go.'

I don't think we've ever moved so fast. The kitchen becomes a hive of activity and Lance phones his men to see who will work on a Sunday. "For double pay", I overhear him telling one of them, and it reminds me again that we owe Lance far more than we can ever repay. And not just in a monetary sense.

'Don't worry, Harriet,' he says, when he catches me looking at him. 'We'll get it done in time no matter what the weather throws at us.' He smiles, walks towards the door, stops and looks back at me, as if he knows I'm still watching him. 'If I were your boyfriend, a few blizzards and a bit of ice wouldn't stop me getting to you. Nothing would stop me being by your side if I thought that's where you wanted me to be.'

I can only just hear that part because he's a few feet away now, and Dad is explaining rather loudly to Reece that an ordinary saw will work equally as well as a chain saw and the twins are pretending to *be* chain saws, but I think that's the nicest thing he's ever said to me and I can't help but wonder exactly what he means. Is he simply being reassuring and telling me that Art will get here? Or is he telling me, in a roundabout way, that he would make his way through blizzards and ice to be with me? That he wants to be with me. I only have to let him know that's where I want him to be? Or am I overthinking a simple, throwaway line?

Chapter Twenty-Eight

I reluctantly lift my hand from beneath the duvet to answer my ringing phone, which Ralph, thoughtfully, has set to play Christmas tunes. At least, unlike the doorbell, I can tell that this one is *We Wish You a Merry Christmas*.

'Morning, Harri.'

I hadn't bothered to see who was calling but I recognise Art's voice immediately.

'Oh hi.' I can hear the mixture of guilt and surprise in my voice so I'm sure he can. I was in the middle of a dream when the phone rang, and in the dream I was having mad, passionate sex. But I wasn't having it with Art. It was Lance I was with and we were rolling around on a fur rug in a rather beautiful, cathedral-like building made of ice.

'I've got a surprise for you,' Art informs me. He sounds decidedly 'chipper'.

I think I may have a surprise for *him*, but this isn't the time to tell him.

'Oh. What sort of surprise?' I try to sound as enthusiastic as I can.

'We've heard the news, and I've spoken with Mum. I've spent the entire day on the phone, because Mum's far too busy, Dad's hopeless at organising anything, and Morgana has never made her own travel arrangements, so she wouldn't know where to start. But it's all settled now.'

I drag myself up to a sitting position. 'I'm sorry. Have I missed something? I'm not following you at all. What do you mean? What travel arrangements? What's all settled now? Are you… are you phoning to tell me you're not coming?'

'What? Of course not. Would I sound so happy if I were phoning to say my family and I won't be spending Christmas at The Hall?'

'Um. No. I suppose you wouldn't. What are you phoning to tell me then?'

'That we've heard about the blizzards, and we were concerned that if there really is the amount of snow they predict, we might not be able to get there on Friday. So I've spoken to Mum and I've rearranged everything. I'm taking the afternoon flight tomorrow and I'll be arriving at Heathrow on Wednesday, around five in the morning. Mum, Dad and Morgana are driving to Heathrow on Tuesday and spending the night and then we'll all drive down to you on Wednesday morning and we should be arriving around ten or eleven. Isn't that wonderful?'

'Shit! I mean… yes. Yes that's… wonderful.' I look at my watch and unless it's stopped again, it's eight a.m. on Monday morning which means it's seven p.m. on Monday evening in Sydney. 'You've rearranged your flight, and you'll all be arriving here on Wednesday morning around ten. Two days early. Is that what you're telling me?'

'Yep. I can't wait to see The Hall. We're all really excited. Spending Christmas in an English stately home is probably on everyone's Christmas wish list, isn't it?'

'Um. I'm not sure what you're expecting, Art. I've shown you photos. You've seen what it's like. I hope your family don't think it looks anything like Highclere Castle. I know your mum and Morgana were big fans of *Downton Abbey*. The Hall is nothing like that. I've told you this before. It's a Tudor Manor house with seventeenth-century additions. It's not a sprawling or magnificent stately home. Please believe me.'

'Oh, Harri. Don't be silly. We know The Hall isn't quite as grand as that, but it's still pretty big, isn't it? And impressive. Anyway, I'd better go and start packing. I've got a lot to do before my flight tomorrow. See you soon. Love you.'

'Art, I really…' He's rung off.

I think I'm about to have heart attack. Or at the very least, a panic attack. Two days. Art and the rest of the Camlan-Browns will be here in just two days.

Oh. My. God.

I jump out of bed and race downstairs and I don't even stop to put my slippers on. Everyone is already in the kitchen when I burst in.

'They've changed their plans. They've heard about the blizzards. They'll be here in two days. At ten in the morning. On Wednesday. This Wednesday!'

'What?' Bella looks as surprised as me.

'Good of them to ask if we mind them arriving early,' Aunt Vicki says.

'All of them?' Merrion asks. 'Art, too?'

I nod in a maniacal fashion. My head feels like one of those hammer drills, Lance's men have been using.

'Yes. He's managed to change his flight. He's just called to tell me. He's leaving tomorrow and his flight arrives at five a.m. on Wednesday.'

'Well, I'm not going to pick him up,' Merrion says. 'But you can borrow my car if you want to.'

'No need. His family are meeting him at Heathrow and they're all travelling here together.'

Bella hands me a mug of coffee and gives me a hug. As she squeezes me tight, I see Lance. He's leaning against the worktop near the window overlooking the kitchen garden. And he looks about as pleased by the news as I am.

He pushes himself upright. 'In that case I'd better get on. I'll see if any of my men can work through the night. That way, there's a chance it'll all be ready in time.'

I drop onto a chair and a long, slow sigh escapes me. I feel exhausted, and strangely deflated. A bit like a little girl who's just been told that Santa won't be coming this year.

Thor tugs my sleeve as Theo clambers onto my lap.

'Why are you sad, Hairy?' Thor asks.

'Do you want a hug?' Theo offers before I have a chance to reply. 'Mummy hugs us if we are sad.'

'Don't you want to see your boyfriend?' Thor asks, hugging my arm.

'Yes,' I say. 'Yes, of course I want to see him.' I smile as Theo slides his hands around my neck and tries to hug me. 'Thanks,' I croak. 'That's a little tight.' I suppose I shouldn't really complain that, in fact, he's nearly strangling me.

Lance, who is on his way to the door, gives me a strange look before he grabs Theo around the waist and lifts him from me. He raises Thor off the ground by his arm.

'Come on you two. I'll need your help if we're going to get everything done by Wednesday morning. And Harriet needs to go and get dressed.'

I meet his eyes for a single moment before realising I'm wearing my brushed cotton pyjamas with snowmen and robins plastered all over them. I must look oh so sexy and alluring – Not!

And once again, Lance and every single member of my family, including the twins, swing into action – apart from me. I just sit there and drink my coffee. I need it. In fact I'm almost tempted to add some of Aunt Vicki's Christmas Cocktail to it. I could probably use some alcohol right now.

Chapter Twenty-Nine

It's eight o'clock on Tuesday night and I'm so exhausted that I'm actually considering putting Art in the Opal Room, regardless of whether or not we fall out. I'm definitely too tired to have sex, no matter how much I've missed it. I'm almost too tired to speak and I seem to be having trouble stringing coherent sentences together.

During the last two days my family and I have barely stopped to eat, let alone sleep. If we were offered parts in a movie to play flesh-eating zombies, right now, we could do so realistically and probably without very much special effects make-up.

The only person who has had any rest at all during the daytime, and slept for more than four hours each night, is Bella, and that is only because we all insisted she must. Even Aunt Vicki has been working like a Trojan. She's dusted and polished every picture, ornament, vase, or any other inanimate object to be found on the ground floor of

The Hall, before working her way up the staircase and onwards to the Long Gallery and the Camlan-Brown's bedrooms and bathrooms. I honestly don't know where she gets the energy from. I just hope I'm able to do what she has when I'm her age.

Lance comes into the kitchen and he looks even more exhausted than me. But he has been working twice as hard, and probably three times faster than the rest of us. And driving home afterwards. Bella told him he should spend last night at The Hall, but he politely declined the offer. I know he didn't leave until three a.m. because I was still up, and I saw him. He was back again by six-thirty, so I'm not sure why he bothered. He could just as easily have stayed here for three and a half hours.

'It's done,' he says, stifling a yawn. 'The Hall is looking as good as it possibly can in such a limited time frame, and it's ready to receive your boyfriend and his family. Do you want to come and look before we switch the floodlights off and go home?'

He doesn't wait for my reply; he turns and leaves the way he came, obviously assuming I'll follow him. Which naturally I do. I may be exhausted but I do want to see what it looks like after all our hard work.

'It's very cold outside,' Lance says, without a backward glance. 'You'll need a coat.'

I go to the cloakroom and put on the warmest coat I can find before hurrying outside after him.

All my family are there – apart from Bella and the twins, who we persuaded to get some sleep an hour or so earlier. They're all standing in a line, along with Lance's men, staring up at the floodlit building.

I walk down the stone steps to join them and when I turn around and look at The Hall, sitting proudly beneath the cold, white glare of the floodlights, it takes my breath away. It may not be a replica of *Downton Abbey* but it looks absolutely magnificent. It probably looks almost as good as the day it was built, but as a great deal of the façade has had to be re-plastered, I suppose most of it is as new as it was more than five hundred years ago.

I can feel the tears in my eyes when I look at Lance.

'I don't know how we will ever thank you, Lance,' I say. 'The Hall has never looked as beautiful.'

'You're right about that,' Dad agrees. 'We all owe you far more than money, Lance. And no matter what you say, I know we owe you a great deal of that. My family and I will be indebted to you for the rest of our lives, and far more than in merely a financial sense.'

Lance shakes his head and smiles. 'It's been a pleasure. I've enjoyed every minute of it. Even the last two days.'

Ralph pats him on the back. 'I bet you're glad though that it's over.'

'Oddly enough, I'm not.' Lance glances at me. 'Do you want to see it with the floodlights off and the Christmas lights on? I believe you'll think it's even more beautiful.'

'Oh, yes please! I can't wait to see it.'

I'm already happy with the way it looks but I can tell from the number of unlit bulbs dangling from row upon row of deftly hidden wires, it will look amazing once they're lit. The massive Christmas tree, Lance and his men planted, stands to one side of us and that too, has enough bulbs to produce a magnificent display.

'We'll just wait a second for Bella and the twins,' he says. 'They should be down any moment. Reece told them we were having a big 'switch on'. I thought they wouldn't want to miss it.'

'I hope they hurry up,' Aunt Vicki grumbles, but she's smiling. 'A person could freeze to death out here. I don't know about blizzards. It feels as if we may be heading for another Ice Age.'

She's right about that. It is absolutely freezing. But as I look up at the sky, and a half-full, waning moon, there isn't a cloud blocking out the myriad stars sparkling like a million diamonds, and not even a breath of wind lifts a strand of Lance's thick, black hair.

'It doesn't look like we'll have snow,' I say. 'Let alone blizzards.'

'Sometimes looks can be deceiving,' Merrion says. 'And if Art and his family aren't impressed by this place, I suggest you dump him immediately and move back home.'

'She should do that anyway,' Aunt Vicki states.

'Tonight isn't about me. It's about The Hall. And about the miracle transformation that Lance and his men have performed.'

'You're right,' Merrion says. 'I think it calls for a celebration. Ralph, come and help me get some champagne and glasses.'

One of Lance's men pipes up: 'Don't suppose I could toast the place with coffee instead, could I, love? It's bloody freezing out here.'

'Brandy, Merrion,' Dad suggests. 'For those who would rather not have champagne. That'll help warm you up.'

'I'll make coffee,' I offer. 'If you'd prefer that.'

'Brandy sounds good to us, love.' Another of Lance's men agrees.

Merrion, Ralph, Lance and I all dash back inside and get the drinks and glasses. Bella walks down the stairs as we're on our way back out, proceeded by the twins who are running so fast they both trip over and slide across the floor. Which of course, means they spend the next few minutes trying to repeat the process.

Only when everyone has filled glasses of whatever happens to be their preference and Merrion has gone back inside and returned with something fizzy for the twins so that they don't feel left out – and so that they stop shouting at the tops of their lungs that they're old enough to have the same as us – does Lance ask if we're all ready.

'I've got it connected to this by a bypass,' he says, holding the switchbox in the air. 'But all the lights will switch on from just inside the front entrance afterwards. Who wants to do the honours? Harriet?'

I shake my head. 'I think Bella should.'

'No, no,' Bella says. 'This is about you coming home this Christmas and us all being together again. You should do it.'

Everyone nods in agreement and I can see that some of Lance's men are looking at their watches. I have forgotten they obviously have homes and families of their own to get to and their own Christmases to prepare for. I take the switchbox and Lance turns off the floodlights, plunging us all into darkness, barring the single streak of pale moonlight on the grass. With a deep breath and a final smile at Lance, I flick the switch.

I can hardly believe my eyes as row upon row of multi-coloured, twinkling lights, illuminate the façade, and hundreds of reflections dance in the panes as if the windows were made of stained glass. The Christmas tree beside us is also ablaze with coloured lights and a single white star shines proudly at the tip.

Every single one of us gasps in delight, including Lance, who looks down at me and smiles as if even he is surprised at how fabulous the display has turned out.

'Cheers!' Merrion says, raising her champagne glass. 'To Christmas, to Harri and to The Hall. Oh, and to Lance and his wonderful band of merry men.'

'Cheers!' We all respond.

We stand, admiring the lights and discussing how amazed we all are that the work is finished in time, despite bringing forward the date. Then, one by one, Lance's men say goodbye, wish us all a very Merry Christmas, and start to pack their tools away.

'You must all come back for a drink and some festive nibbles during Christmas,' Bella insists. 'And bring your families, of course.'

'Yes,' Dad agrees.

'What about on Friday night?' Merrion suggests. 'We could have a party. It's the night before Christmas Eve. Wouldn't that be great?'

'The last time we had a party,' Aunt Vicki reminds us, 'was the day before Harriet left.'

Ralph quickly says: 'So this party will be to celebrate her return, as well as to say thank you to Lance and all the men.'

'Party! Party! Party!' Theo and Thor obviously like the idea.

Lance's men all nod, but Lance looks at me and I can see the frown forming.

'Won't your boyfriend and his family mind?'

For a moment I had completely forgotten about my boyfriend – and his family.

'I don't see why they should. Everyone likes a party.'

'But… you may want to celebrate something else. Something more important.'

'What could be more important than Harriet's return?' Aunt Vicki asks.

I swear my aunt has super powers. Lance had lowered his voice to little above a whisper when he said that, but still she heard it. I realise he's referring to the fact that I think Art will propose before Christmas.

'Um. Well, I'm not too sure about that,' I whisper back. In my usual voice I add: 'We can celebrate anything and everything with one big party. I think it's a wonderful idea. And I know there won't be a lack of food. There's enough to see us through this Christmas and the next one from what I've seen.'

Bella looks unsure. 'I may make a few more mince pies, to be on the safe side. And possibly a few more sausage rolls. And perhaps one or two other things, just in case. It's always better to have too much than not enough.'

'That's agreed then,' Dad says. 'We're having a party on Friday night and everyone is invited.'

'I promise I won't blow anything up,' Reece says.

Dad pats him on the shoulder. 'Actually, Reece, for once there's a chance you can, and with our blessing. You know we wanted to do something special for New Year's Eve? Well, Lance and I had a chat, and Lance knows someone, who knows a man who does firework displays. Perhaps we could get him here on Friday instead of New Year's Eve, and you may be allowed to help him.'

'I could make some myself.' Reece sounds exceedingly enthusiastic.

'No, no, Reece,' Bella says. 'I will not allow you in a room on your own with gunpowder. Absolutely not. Lance has only just finished refurbishing The Hall. We certainly don't want to have to ask him to rebuild it from the foundations up.'

Chapter Thirty

Lance's men have now all gone to their respective homes, and only Lance remains. I know this because, yet again, I'm staring out of one of the kitchen front windows, watching him. Once or twice he's looked in my direction but as I quickly darted to one side each time, I'm sure he didn't see me.

Most of my family has long since gone to bed and only Merrion, Ralph and I, are sitting in the kitchen. Merrion is writing a list of things she thinks we need for the party on Friday and Ralph is supposed to be helping, but as he's emptied the contents of an entire bottle of brandy, virtually single-handedly, his suggestions are not terribly helpful. And most of them don't make sense.

'Why don't you go to bed, Ralph?' Merrion snaps.

Ralph grins. 'You going to invite your 'friend'? The car man.'

It's obvious what he means but Merrion pretends she doesn't understand.

'You're about as much help as an alien from another planet, and equally as unintelligible. Go. To. Bed.'

'You watching Lance?' Ralph says, clearly addressing that comment to me.

'No.' I hastily move away from the window. 'I was just admiring the lights. They're so beautiful.'

'Admiring something. Not the lights. Should offer Lance a nightcap.' He gets to his feet and staggers towards the door.

Merrion looks up at me as I return to the window.

'You do know he will probably go and tell Lance you've been watching him, don't you?'

'He won't?'

She nods. 'He will.'

I rush after Ralph but to my great relief, he's making his way upstairs. I stand and watch him, to make sure he doesn't change his mind and go in search of Lance, and only when he disappears along the corridor do I decide it's safe and let out the breath I hadn't realised I was holding.

'I've come to say good night.'

Lance's voice startles me and I spin round in surprise to face him.

'Oh! I thought you'd gone home.'

His lips twitch. 'Did you? I thought you could see that I hadn't.'

'Um. I did see you were still here a while ago, but I've been so mesmerised by the beautiful lights and the incredibly starry sky that I hardly even noticed you.'

'Is that so?'

'Yes. And I was just about to go to bed.'

He nods. 'I'll say good night then.'

'Yes. Good night. And pleasant dreams.'

He doesn't move. He simply stares at me. I stare back, although I don't mean to. I wonder if the twins have covered the floor with glue because I can't seem to move – and I wouldn't put it past them.

'You must be looking forward to tomorrow,' he finally says.

'Yes.'

'I hope all the work's been worth it. Personally, I thought The Hall looked fine as it was.'

'Did you?'

'Yes.'

'But it was falling apart.'

'It's an old building. It was part of its charm.'

'You wouldn't have thought it was very charming if you were sleeping in the bed in the Queen's Room and rain was pouring on your head.'

He grins. 'I suppose not. But we've done more than repair the roof.'

'I know you have. And as Dad said, I honestly don't know how we will ever repay you.'

'There's nothing to repay.'

'Nonsense. I heard you on the phone on Sunday telling your men you would pay them double time. That in itself has put you out of pocket.'

His eyes narrow for a split second before a grin spreads across his face. 'I'm sure someone told me that it was impolite to listen to people's telephone conversations. And I wasn't talking to myself.'

I can't believe he remembers me saying that. 'Yes. Well. That's not the point. The point is we must owe you a considerable amount of money. We haven't even paid you for the Christmas decorations and lights yet.'

'Merrion paid for some of them and the rest I got so cheap that it's hardly worth discussing.'

'Well, at the very least, I think we owe you dinner. I owe you dinner. We should go out to dinner again. When are you free? It's my treat. What about Thursday? Are you free on Thursday?'

He doesn't answer immediately and I wonder if I've gone too far. I think I may have sounded a bit too eager, possibly even desperate.

'I'm not sure your boyfriend would like that.'

I wave my hand in the air in a carefree manner. 'I don't need his permission.'

'No. But he is flying thousands of miles to be with you. To spend Christmas with you. It seems a little rude to tell him that you're going out to dinner with another man the day after he arrives.'

'Oh.' Even I can see that wouldn't go down terribly well. 'Yes. I suppose so.'

We stand in silence for a moment until Merrion appears from the kitchen, looks at both of us and grins.

'Can't bear to say good night? Well, don't mind me. I'm off to bed. Good night, Lance, good luck, Harri. Don't do anything I wouldn't do.' She runs up the stairs before I realise what she said.

Lance looks thoughtful. 'Good luck? Why did she wish you good luck?'

'Oh, you know Merrion. Sometimes she says the silliest things. I have no idea why she said that.'

He tips his head a little to one side and his dark eyes seem to penetrate my soul.

'Don't you? Is there something you want to tell me, Harriet? Something you think I need to know tonight?'

I try to swallow, but I can't and I end up trying to clear my throat with a series of strange, strangled little coughs.

'Are you okay?' He moves towards me.

'Fine,' is all I can manage to say, but I'm finally able to move and I take a few steps back.

He stops, and the expression on his face indicates that he's not quite sure what he should do next.

'I'd better go. Good night, Harriet.'

He turns and walks towards the door, pulls it open with one hand and steps across the threshold.

'Lance!' I rush towards him and he stops just outside the door.

'Yes, Harriet.' I can't see his face now because he's standing in the shadow of the colonnade, but I can hear a note of optimism in those two little words.

I stop just inside the doorway and have no idea what to say or do next. I know I shouldn't have called his name but I couldn't prevent myself from doing so.

'I… I…'

'Yes… Harriet.' He leaves a little space between each word and it sounds as if he's answering an unasked question.

A breeze whips up from nowhere, and the string of lights above us tinkles in the cold night air. The stream of moonlight disappears behind a cloud and I can see the first few snowflakes falling, against the backdrop of the night.

'I… I just want to thank you again for everything you've done. Especially for all of these beautiful lights.' I grin at him. 'You've definitely brightened up my life. All our lives.'

He smiles wanly. 'And your family has brightened mine.'

I wait for him to add the words, "and so have you", but he doesn't. Foolishly, I find that rather annoying.

'But not me? *I* haven't brightened up *your* life? Well, thank you very much.'

'No, Harriet. I wish I could say that you had, because I know for a fact that you could. You could make my life so bright, if you wanted to. But you're not sure if you do. Until you are, one way or the other, I'll feel as if I'm stumbling in the dark.'

I'm not sure what he means by that, but as I'm about to ask, I hear Dad's voice.

'I thought I heard Harri call your name just now, Lance. I've been in my study and I didn't realise the time. I know it's late, but is there any chance I could have a quick word with you before you go?'

Lance looks at me for a second before smiling at Dad. 'Of course, Wyndham.'

'Come back in the warm and have a drink. You don't have to get back to take care of Thunder, do you?'

'No. I left him with the Tarrants again today. He'll be fast asleep on one of their kid's beds, if I know him.'

Dad looks at me. 'You still up, darling? You should get along to bed. I know you women. You'll want to look your best for that boyfriend of yours tomorrow. You should get some sleep. Art's a lucky man, don't you think, Lance?'

'Yes I do. He's a very, very lucky man.'

'Good night, Harri,' Dad says, clearly giving me my marching orders.

There's nothing I can do. I could wait up, but who knows how long Dad will keep Lance talking.

'Good night, Dad. Good night, Lance.'

As Lance closes the door and walks past me towards Dad, I'm sure the look in his eyes is telling me something. I simply don't know what it is.

Dad reaches out his hand to me, and I go towards him. He kisses me on the cheek and brushes a strand of hair from my eyes.

'Good night, my darling. Sleep well. Things are going to be very different around here from tomorrow onwards. It'll be so quiet and relaxing that we won't know what to do with ourselves.'

Chapter Thirty-One

I was sure I wouldn't be able to sleep, but it seems I was wrong.

I decided I would wait up for a while, and if Lance wasn't with Dad for too long, we might be able to pick up where we left off. I came back downstairs, made some coffee, and sat in one of the comfy chairs near the kitchen front windows.

But when I open my eyes and peer out, I can't see Lance's truck, and all the Christmas lights have been switched off.

Lance has gone, and I've missed my chance.

I may as well go to bed. There's nothing else I can do until the morning. Perhaps I'll get a chance to speak to Lance before Art and his family arrive. At least the snow has stopped. There's a dusting on the window sill and a thin blanket on the ground but that's about it.

I'm trudging up the stairs when a thought hits me. Dad said earlier that things will change tomorrow and it'll be quiet and relaxing. It's only now that I realise exactly what he meant. He meant there won't be any builders here. There won't be any need for them to come. The work on The Hall is complete. Does that mean Lance won't be here tomorrow? Well, I suppose it's technically today as it's three a.m., according to the grandfather clock in the Great Hall, which is currently strikingly the hour.

Surely, we'll still see him? Surely, he'll still come round? I've become so used to him being here each day that I took it for granted that would continue. Panic bubbles through my veins and goosebumps prickle my arms.

I have to know. I have to know right now. I have to ask Merrion.

I run to her room, tap on the door and dash inside.

She's fast asleep.

'Merrion! Merrion wake up!'

Merrion shoots up into a sitting position, her startled eyes as wide as saucers, her mouth hanging open in shock.

'Merrion it's me. I need to ask you something.'

She tries to focus her bleary eyes and blinks several times.

'Harri? What's wrong? What's happened? What time is it?'

'It's a little after three o'clock.'

She blinks again. 'In the morning?'

'Yes, of course in the morning. It wouldn't be pitch black out if it was three in the afternoon.'

'Is it Mum? Has something happened to her and the baby?'

'No. Bella's fine. Everyone's fine.'

'Then why in God's name have you woken me up at three o'clock in the morning?'

'If you'll stop asking questions, I'll tell you.'

'Okay. Tell me. And it had better be a matter of life or death, or you won't live to see your boyfriend and his family arrive.'

'It's Lance. He's gone.'

She sighs dramatically. 'It's three o'clock in the morning and the work's finished. Of course he's gone. Wait a minute. You do just mean gone home, don't you? Not, gone as in, *gone*.'

'Yes. Well no. I mean. I don't think he's *gone*, exactly. I just don't know when he's coming back. And I need to. I need to know when I'll see him again. We were in the middle of a conversation and Dad interrupted.'

Merrion screws up her eyes and shakes her head.

'Harri, I have no idea what you're talking about. Are you seriously telling me that you've woken me up at this godforsaken hour to tell me you need to finish a conversation with Lance?'

'Yes. It was an important conversation.'

I can see by her face that I've finally got her attention.

'Important as in *important*? As in, you were finally going to tell each other how you feel?'

'Yes, I… Hold on. What d'you mean by "tell each other" and "finally"? What's "finally" supposed to mean?'

She sighs and slaps me on my arm. 'You are such an idiot sometimes, Harri. It was pretty obvious to me that Lance liked you the minute he laid eyes on you. And it was also fairly obvious that you thought he looked rather good.'

'What?'

'Oh come on. Don't pretend. It's me you're talking to.'

'Does anyone else think that?'

Merrion shrugs. 'Ralph absolutely does. Aunt Vicki, almost certainly. Dad, absolutely not. Mum, possibly. Reece? Well, I have no idea what Reece thinks. Ever. And the twins? No one cares what they think. At least I don't.'

I drop down onto her bed. 'What should I do, Merrion? My boyfriend and his family arrive in less than seven hours. I love Art. I know I do, and yet all I can think about is telling Lance that I would really like the opportunity to see if I could brighten his life.'

'To see if you could do what? Lance has a pretty good life. It doesn't need brightening. He's happy. At least, he was. Oh. Is 'brightening his life' an Australian euphemism for having sex with him?'

'What? No, of course it isn't. We were having a conversation about the lights. The Christmas lights. I thanked him for brightening up my life with the Christmas lights. And he told me that my family brightened up his. But he didn't say that I did. Although he did say I could if I wanted to. But he wasn't sure I wanted to. And that's when Dad interrupted. So Lance doesn't know that I would like the opportunity to brighten up his life.'

'With… Christmas… lights? I bloody well hope that *is* some sort of code for having sex or at least for kissing, because if you're seriously telling me that you have woken me up at three o'clock in the morning to talk about Christmas lights, you really are dead.'

'Of course it's not about Christmas lights. It's about going out to dinner.'

'You're still dead.'

'About going out on a date together.'

'You're half dead.'

'About telling him that I think I've fallen in love with him, and hoping that he feels the same about me.'

'Halle-bloody-lujah! Finally.'

'So what do I do? I've fallen in love with a man I've known for less than a fortnight, and my boyfriend of almost two years is arriving in seven hours, to propose. I think. What do I say to him? What should I say to Lance?'

'You're asking me? You're seriously asking me? You're the elder sister. I'm supposed to come to you for advice on love, sex and all that stuff, not the other way around. And you've got a boyfriend. All I've got is a rich friend who likes to buy me stuff. And no, don't look at me like that. He is just a friend. Simply a friend. He's merely very, very rich. So rich that buying me that car was the equivalent of me buying the twins one of those tiny, toy cars they insist on rolling across the floor in front of me. So there's no point in asking me. You need to ask Mum. She'll know what to do. But not at three o'clock in the morning.'

I glance at my watch and open my mouth to speak but she stops me.

'No. I don't care if it is later than three. You are *not* waking Mum up until at least eight o'clock.'

'Seven?' I venture. 'Don't give me that look. Bella's always up early.'

'If she's downstairs at seven, you can ask her. But you are not waking her up until eight. Promise me. Lance isn't going anywhere until Christmas Eve.'

'Okay, I promise. Wait a minute. What do you mean? He isn't going anywhere until Christmas Eve? Where's he going on Christmas Eve?'

Her eyes open wide. 'Didn't he tell you tonight? I thought that's what all the panic was about. I assumed that's why you felt you needed to speak to him so urgently.'

'Where's he going, Merrion?'

'Don't panic. He's coming back.'

'Where's he going?'

She grins. 'Don't get stroppy. It's actually quite amazing. He only decided yesterday. He's going to Aspen to spend Christmas with his sisters.'

I'm a little relieved. But not entirely. I don't want him to go anywhere. At least not before talking to me.

'And when's he coming back?'

She shrugs. 'The New Year, I think. He didn't really say. He said that it depends what happens over Christmas. But you don't seem to realise why the fact that he's going is so amazing.'

'Okay. Aspen is amazing. Big deal.'

'No. Not that he's going to Aspen. That he's going by plane. He's flying.'

I laugh at that. 'Of course he's flying. He could hardly get to Aspen from here without flying.'

She leans towards me and looks me directly in the eye. 'But that's the point. That's why he was going to be spending Christmas with us. Why he spent Christmas with us last year. And the first year he was here, just after you had left.'

'He was going to be spending Christmas with us? No one told me that. No one tells me anything. Why isn't he going to be now? Why has he suddenly decided to go to Aspen?'

Merrion jumps onto her knees, grabs me by the arms and shakes me.

'Harri! He's decided to go to Aspen because he doesn't want to be here when your idiot boyfriend asks you to marry him. And if Art does, and you're stupid enough to say yes, then Lance probably won't come back until you've returned to Australia. If he comes back at all. Although I'm sure he will, because of Thunder. He might leave his dog for a few weeks, but he definitely wouldn't leave him here permanently.'

I can't believe what I'm hearing.

'Merrion, please. My head is spinning and I really don't understand what's going on. Are you honestly saying that Lance is going to Aspen because he's jealous? Because he can't bear the thought of being here if Art proposes to me?'

She nods frantically. 'Yes!'

'How do you know this?'

'Because I know Lance. I know him really well. And also because he told Ralph most of that, and Ralph told me.'

'Why didn't Ralph tell me? Why doesn't *anyone* in this family *ever* tell me anything?'

'I think that's my fault. I was absolutely certain that Lance would say something to you tonight. I was convinced of it. So I told Ralph not to interfere.'

'Oh dear God.' I remember something she said earlier. 'Why did you make such a big deal about Lance flying, by the way?'

'I thought you said you're in love with him? Don't you know anything about the man?'

'Apparently not.' I'm getting a little tired of her.

'He's frightened of flying. Terrified. Scared to death.'

I laugh at that. Until I see she's serious.

'You are joking?'

'Nope. But he's so determined not to spend Christmas here. And obviously, he knows we won't let him spend Christmas on his own if he stays in the village. Plus, he doesn't have an excuse to be anywhere else. And he probably doesn't want to be alone anyway. So Aspen is his only option. He told Ralph that he needs to do it anyway at some stage. Because he can't be terrified of it for the rest of his life. So he decided Christmas Eve was as good a time as any.'

And as incredible as that is, and in spite of the fact that Merrion has just told me that Lance feels the same way about me as I do about him, the thing I find the most amazing is that Lance is afraid of flying. Not that it makes the slightest difference to the way I feel, of course. If anything, it makes me love him a little more. I was beginning to think that nothing could get to him. That nothing would give him pause. It's oddly comforting to know that he's as vulnerable as the rest of us. But it's not in the least bit comforting to know that he's going to Aspen on Christmas Eve. And he's going because of me.

Chapter Thirty-Two

Wednesday morning does not get off to a good start.

I wake up on Merrion's bed, and when I check my watch I see it's already nine o'clock. Merrion is fast asleep, and so it seems is everyone else. I can't even hear the twins. There's nothing but silence. I jump to my feet, shake Merrion awake, and as I run to the window and pull the curtains open, there is nothing but snow outside. The blizzards must have arrived while we all slept in our beds. Well, I slept on Merrion's bed, but that hardly matters.

There's not a breath of wind by the looks of it and it's as silent as the grave out there right now. Large white flakes of snow are falling as softly as the contents of a million goose down duvets, landing feather-like onto the layer of snow already on the ground.

'You still here?' Merrion says. 'What time is it?'

'It's nine. And I don't think anyone is up yet. Art and his family will be here soon. And I can't see Lance's truck.'

Merrion rubs her eyes and peers at the window. 'Is that snow? Or am I so tired that I'm seeing long white lines in front of my eyes.'

'It's snow. It's falling so thick and fast that it's like a curtain out there. I think there's already a foot or so on the ground.'

'Well, that solves one of your problems. Art and his family may not be able to get here, after all.'

'They might. It depends what time it began snowing like this. It might not have started until after his plane landed. All the major roads will have been gritted so there's every possibility Art and his family are already on their way. They may be delayed, but they'll get here. Art is so determined, I know he'll find a way.'

Merrion sighs. 'I suppose I'd better get up then.'

'I wonder why he hasn't called.'

'Where's your phone.'

'It's beside the bed. I left it there last night when I went back down to the kitchen.' I nod towards the bedside table. Except it's not, of course, *my* bedside table. 'Oh bugger! It's in my room.'

I race along the corridor and Merrion yells after me that she'll see me in the kitchen. I reach my room and grab my phone. There are six text messages and four missed calls. And they're all from Art. I hold my breath and call him.

'Where the hell have you been, Harri? I've been trying to get hold of you for hours.'

He isn't pleased. I suppose I can't blame him.

'Um. Yeah. Sorry about that. I fell asleep in Merrion's room. I forgot I'd left my phone in mine. I also overslept.'

'Great. I've just flown thousands of miles and you've overslept.'

'I said I'm sorry, Art. It's been a very… tiring week. Um. You're here then? In England? Your flight wasn't cancelled?'

'Yes, I'm here. We're all here. Although none of us know exactly where *here* is. We can't see a damned thing. There were horrendous delays on the M25 and now we're… somewhere between that and Hall's Cross. According to the satnav, we're thirty miles from our destination.'

'Only thirty miles? That isn't very far at all.'

'Perhaps not to you. But when you're stuck in a car and surrounded by snow, and you can't see the road let alone a signpost, it feels like a bloody long way from any form of civilisation.'

'I see. Um. So… when do you think you'll get here?'

Art tuts. 'I've just told you, Harri. I don't know where we are, so I don't know when we'll get to you. If we ever get to you, that is. We may be trapped in this snow for hours.'

'They did forecast blizzards.'

'Yes. Thanks for pointing that out. That's really very helpful.'

'Don't get mad at me. You were the one who decided to change your flight and arrive today.'

'You're right. I'm sorry. It's just so annoying, that's all.'

'I understand. Um. The satnav should be able to tell you where you currently are and if you give me the postcode or whatever, I'll ask Dad or Ralph to give you directions. I may be able to, but I noticed on my way here that some of the roads had changed over the last two years. It's better if I ask them. Only… I don't think they're up yet. Art? Art are you still there?'

'Yes. I was just a little surprised that you and your family seem to still be in bed at nine fifteen in the morning. Especially as you're expecting us.'

He's got a point. 'We're all usually up extremely early, Art. It's just that, as I said, it's been a tiring week.'

'Yes. Well. Will you please go and see if your dad and stepbrother are up? The sooner someone tells us where we are, the sooner we'll be there with you.'

'I'll go and find Dad right away and I'll call you back. I won't be long, I promise.'

'Good. Speak very soon then. Bye.'

I ring off and go in search of Dad but before I reach his room, I'm sure I hear the engine of a truck outside. It sounds like Lance's truck. I race downstairs without thinking and run to the front doors – which of course I can't get open. I call Lance's name but there's no reply. There's nothing else for it. I'll have to go via the kitchen.

I dash into the kitchen, have sense enough to realise that, although I didn't get undressed last night and therefore still have my clothes on, it's probably freezing outside. I run and grab a coat from the cloakroom, then race across the utility room and out into thick, deep snow. I trudge my way around the kitchen garden to the front of The Hall.

I can't see Lance, and what's more, I can't see a truck. All I can see is snow. And it's halfway up my shins. I hear the engine again and look around me, twisting and turning this way and that, but still all I can see is snow. Sounds must be travelling in the air or something. There's clearly no one here.

I trudge back inside, shake of clumps of icy snow and go to the kitchen. I'll make coffee and get breakfast started before I go upstairs to shower and change. Everyone should be getting up soon because Merrion will no doubt have woken them to tell… Oh bugger it! I've completely forgotten about Art.

I reach into my pocket to retrieve my phone and I'm just about to call him when I see he's calling me.

'Sorry, Art,' I say before he has a chance to speak. 'I'm still looking for Dad. He must be up and about somewhere. I'll call you back the second I find him. Bye.' I ring off and go in search of Dad, or Ralph, or anyone who may be able to tell Art where he is and how to get from there to here. If

Lance was here, he'd know. Or he'd know someone else who would.

I can already tell. It's going to be one of those days.

Chapter Thirty-Three

Dad was wrong. So far today has been anything *but* quiet and relaxing. We've all been running around like the proverbial headless chicken. Or perhaps that should be turkey, bearing in mind it's the festive season.

Neither Dad or Ralph, surprisingly, could tell Art how to get to The Hall. But Merrion could. She even offered to misdirect them for me and send Art and his family thirty miles further away in the other direction, but naturally, I said no.

'Depending on how well Art can follow my instructions', she said, 'and ignore his satnav, and of course whether the snow gets any worse, the Camlan-Browns should be with us somewhere between ten-thirty and twelve. It'll probably take them longer because of the conditions but if some of the roads have been cleared, they may get here sooner, so I can't give you an accurate time.'

Which basically meant we had no idea when to expect them, and as it turns out, her estimate is way off track. It's now one o'clock, and there's still no sign of their arrival. What's more, I can't seem to get through to Art on the phone. My calls go to voicemail and my texts remain unanswered.

'Are you sure you didn't direct them via Devil's Head Drop?' Ralph asks Merrion as we sit down to a buffet lunch. 'And they've driven off the cliff.'

'I didn't even think of telling them to go that way,' she replies, the light in her eyes suggesting that she almost wishes she had.

The road to Devil's Head Drop is notorious for accidents even in good weather when the skies are clear and one can actually see what's in front of them, so today, I would imagine it's been closed off.

Panic is beginning to set in. It's started snowing again and the wind is picking up. I can't help worrying whether something awful has happened, and as ridiculous as it sounds, I have just suggested to Merrion that perhaps we should go and look for them.

'Are you totally insane? I wouldn't go out in this weather to look for you, so I'm certainly not going out to look for them. Besides, I heard on the radio that another blizzard is on the way. The authorities are advising people to stay indoors and not to venture out for anything other than emergencies.'

'This *is* an emergency,' I inform her.

'I'm sure they're fine,' Bella says, giving me a reassuring hug.

It doesn't help. And neither does one chicken breast, two sausage rolls, three mince pies, four

Christmas cookies and a few portions of trifle. Nor do several glasses of wine, followed by a mug of hot chocolate topped with cream and sprinkled with marshmallows. Nothing helps.

I'm starting to send myself on a guilt trip. Art and his family are somewhere out there, lost in the snow, like Scott's doomed expedition in the Antarctic, and it's all because of me. This is the price I'm paying for being 'mentally' unfaithful to my boyfriend. I dread to think what the price would have been if I had also been physically unfaithful.

We're now all huddled on the sofas in the sitting room, drinking more hot chocolate, and wondering what to do next when Reece jumps up and rushes to the window.

'I thought I heard Lance's truck,' he says.

'It's the weather playing tricks on you,' I tell him. 'I thought I heard it earlier, but it was nowhere in sight.'

'I can see it. And I can see Lance.'

I scramble to my feet and run to the window. He's right. It is Lance's truck slowly making its way up the drive. I turn from the window and head towards the door.

'I think we can all stop wondering what's happened to the Camlan-Browns,' Reece adds, as I reach the sitting room door. 'Unless I'm very much mistaken, I think they're in the car which seems to be attached to a rope tied to the back of Lance's truck.

I run back to the window and peer out. Once again he's right. I can just see Art's face through the windscreen of the car behind the truck, as the wipers battle to clear the increasingly heavy amount of falling snow.

Merrion comes and links her arm through mine. 'Now isn't this a curious turn of events? Who'd have thought that Lance would be the one to bring your boyfriend safely to our door? I wonder if he was in the least bit tempted to take the road to Devil's Head Drop.'

Bella comes to the window too. 'Why would anyone take that road on a day like this? Besides it's probably been closed off. We'd better go and greet our guests. And make lots more hot chocolate I should think.'

We all walk towards the front doors and with help from Ralph and Reece, Dad manages to get one of them open.

'We should have asked Lance to hang new doors,' Dad says, shaking his head.

Lance has just got out of his truck and Thunder is jumping up and down beside him as if the dog's attached to a spring; one minute he's visible, the next he's head deep in a pile of snow and all I can see are his ears. Instead of coming to the door, Lance walks towards the car he's towed, untying the rope along the way.

Art gets out, and pulling a face, steps into the knee deep snow. His dad opens the rear door and helps Art's mum who looks even less pleased than

Art. To my surprise, Lance opens the other rear door and I see a pair of long, perfectly shaped legs leading to a short coat which, even in this freezing weather, is open at the front to reveal an even shorter skirt. This is followed by possibly the most lustrous, ice-blonde long flowing hair that I have ever seen surrounding a face an angel would envy, with Cupid's-bow red lips, and lashes so long I can see them from here. This, I assume, is Morgana, Art's twenty-eight-year-old sister and to say that she is stunning is doing her an injustice. She didn't look like this on the few occasions we've exchanged brief greetings via Skype or Facetime.

And just when I thought today couldn't possibly get worse, Lance smiles at her, as if the sun has come out and brightened his world, and to top it off, he only goes and sweeps her up into his arms to carry her across the snow.

I'm not sure I like him, after all.

Morgana giggles, and I can hear her say: 'Oh, Lance. You're so strong.'

'Nonsense,' Lance says, looking just like Thunder does when Lance gives him a dog treat. 'You're as light as a feather.'

I've definitely taken an instant dislike to Morgana.

'Oh my God.' Merrion squeezes my hand. 'I think you may have competition.'

'Bloody hell,' Ralph says. 'You didn't tell us Morgana looked like that. She's drop-dead gorgeous.'

Merrion adds: 'Are those boobs real? Lance may end up with a black eye. Or two black eyes.'

And Reece only makes things worse. 'I wonder if she's at all interested in chemistry. She could come to my room and I'll show her some of my experiments.'

I'm almost beginning to wish the Camlan-Browns were still lost in the snow.

Chapter Thirty-Four

'Welcome to our home,' Dad says, smiling and opening his arms, both literally and figuratively, to Art and his family.

Art looks as if he's been taken to the servant's quarters instead of the stately home he's been expecting. His dad, Phillip smiles directly at Merrion as if he'd like to find her in his Christmas stocking. And Morgana's too busy fluttering her eyelashes at Lance to even notice The Hall, or any of us. Camilla's face is as flat and expressionless as a floorboard but her eyes let me know quite clearly that she's definitely *not* impressed. I'm not sure if it's me or The Hall she doesn't like the look of, but I have an unpleasant feeling it's both.

'How… very… quaint, The Hall is,' she says, as Dad takes her hand. 'I must admit I was expecting it to be… larger. A little more… grand, perhaps. More like those marvellous stately homes one sees on the TV on Sunday evenings. Not that I have time to *watch* TV, of course. I'm far too busy appearing *on* TV to have time in my hectic schedule for that.'

When Dad pulls her towards him and kisses her cheek, she looks truly horrified, and when Bella goes to do the same, she grabs Art by the sleeve of his coat and yanks him between her and Bella.

'We've been so worried about you,' Bella says.

'Your phone doesn't seem to be working,' I say to Art, as I step forward to greet him. 'Where have you been?'

He gives me a quick peck on the lips. 'Stuck in a bank of snow just outside the village. If you can call that place a village. We didn't even know it was there until this man came along and helped us get the car out of the snow. It wouldn't start so he towed us here. He says he knows you.'

Lance gently deposits Morgana on her feet as if he's worried she may break if he sets her down too quickly.

'I'd been to see someone who may have new hinges for your front doors and was on my way back when I spotted the car,' he tells Dad, completely ignoring me. 'They'd driven off the road.'

'We couldn't *see* the road,' Art says.

'We're so lucky you came to our rescue, Laaaaance.' Morgana strings out his name as if she's savouring it... with her tongue. 'And that you had some rope to tie to our car. Do you always have rope... Laaaaance?'

If that's not a suggestive remark, I don't know what is, and I can tell from the look Lance is giving her that he thinks so too. He smiles at her in a way he's never smiled at me. It's positively… debauched.

Camilla grabs her and wraps an arm around her shoulders. 'We're all exceedingly grateful to the man, I'm sure. This is my daughter, Morgana.' Camilla displays her in front of us and Morgana flicks her ice-blonde hair, and darts a seductive look at Lance.

I take Morgana's perfectly manicured hand and yank it, along with her and her bright red talons towards me.

'It's wonderful to finally meet you in the flesh,' I say, and I notice her shoot another look at Lance when I say those last three words. Dear God, if the woman ripped off her tightly fitting, open-necked blouse, dropped her, undoubtedly lace, knickers, and lay spread-eagled on the cold, hard, stone floor of the colonnade she could hardly make it more obvious.

'Oh yes. Likewise.'

Well, that was certainly effusive.

'Come in, come in,' Bella says. 'We'll finish the introductions in the warm. We don't want to be standing around here in the cold and snow for long.'

'You shouldn't be standing in it at all,' Aunt Vicki pipes up. 'Not in your condition.'

'Condition?' Camilla looks horrified and takes a step back, pulling Morgana with her. 'It's nothing catching is it?'

Bella smiles. 'No. It's definitely not catching.'

'But you're unwell?' Camilla clearly wants to be sure she's not going to pick up something unpleasant.

Bella shakes her head. 'I'm absolutely fine. I don't know why Vicki even mentioned it. I'm pregnant, that's all.'

'Pregnant!' Camilla's even more horrified by that. 'At your age?'

She looks Bella up and down and her lip actually curls. I swear it does. When she looks at me, it curls a little more.

'I had no idea your family was so... fertile.'

'Mum,' Art says, wrapping his arms around me and effectively pinning my arms to my sides – which is just as well. I'm tempted to push his mother down the steps. 'You're such a tease. I'm not sure Harri and her family will understand your sense of humour.'

I don't think anyone would understand it because there's nothing teasing or humorous about any of the things she's said or the way she's behaved. It's clear the woman doesn't have a sense of humour. It's also clear she doesn't have any manners, either.

'Are you coming in or not?' Aunt Vicki snaps. 'It's cold. We want to shut the doors.'

'Welcome to The Hall,' Merrion says. 'We're all *so thrilled* to have you here.'

Now that is humour I *do* understand. Although some would call it sarcasm.

Chapter Thirty-Five

It's been a peculiar couple of hours. The Camlan-Browns came in, although I think I can honestly say that if it hadn't been for the blizzard and the fact that Camilla knew their car wouldn't start, she would have tried to find a way to leave. I don't think she smiled once, and the more she saw of the interior of The Hall, the more horror-stricken she became, especially when she saw the bedrooms.

'*This* is the Queen's Room?'

She stood at the doorway and wouldn't go inside for several minutes, until I told her it was the best bedroom in The Hall.

Art wasn't particularly enamoured by his bedroom either.

'I thought I'd be sleeping in your room,' he said, when I took him to the Opal Room.

'I know. But Dad's a bit old-fashioned and as for Aunt Vicki, well, she'd have a heart attack if she thought you and I were sharing a room.'

I shouldn't tell lies, I know, but sometimes it's necessary.

'You told me they weren't old-fashioned,' Art persisted, reaching out to me. But I deftly sidestepped his advance.

'Did I? In most things they're not. But when it comes to sex, it seems they are. I'd obviously forgotten.'

'But they know we live together in Australia.' He reached out again and this time he managed to pull me into his arms. But I managed to ease myself away.

'Yes. But that's on the other side of the world. What the eye doesn't see, and all that. They just don't want single people having sex under their roof. Oh, and you'd better tell Morgana that.'

'Why would Morgana need to know that? You're not making any sense, Harri.'

'I'm very tired. And that's another reason why having separate rooms is good. I'm far too tired for sex and I wouldn't want to get your hopes up.'

'There's not much chance of getting anything up, the way you're behaving.'

Poor Art. I almost felt guilty. But not quite. I needed a bit of breathing space. I needed time to think.

I went downstairs in the hope that I might get a chance to speak to Lance. To see why he was behaving strangely. But when I got to the sitting room, I saw Morgana had got there first, so I went in search of Bella. She was in the kitchen with

Merrion and was staring at a bottle of champagne as if she could really murder a drink.

'They don't seem very... pleased to be here,' Bella said.

'They don't seem very nice,' Merrion added. 'And is Morgana a prostitute or something? Because she certainly looks and behaves like one.'

'Now who's not being very nice?' I said.

Bella nodded. 'They're probably just tired. I'm sure they'll feel better once they've settled in.

But they didn't. If anything, they became worse.

Camilla came back downstairs and seemed surprised to find Lance was still with us – and was seated on one of the sofas in the sitting room chatting amiably to Aunt Vicki.

'Oh. You're still here,' she said, scrunching up her nose as if he were a nasty smell.

When he replied that he was, and he was joining us for drinks and nibbles, at Bella and Wyndham's insistence, I seriously thought Camilla would faint from the shock of it.

And later, when both Bella and Dad, along with the rest of my family, insisted Lance should also stay for dinner, I was worried that Camilla might have a stroke. Morgana, on the other hand, seemed delighted on both counts and I couldn't help but notice that she took every opportunity she could to either touch Lance with her hands, brush her voluptuous breasts against his body, and even on one occasion, to 'accidentally' fall onto his lap. And she certainly took her time to get off it. Lance even had to help her up.

I definitely don't like Morgana.

It's also becoming painfully clear that Lance isn't the man I thought he was. He's hardly looked at me since he arrived and he hasn't said one word to me. Not one. Not even hello.

The only highlight was this evening when we came back into the sitting room after dinner and Morgana bent forward in front of Lance.

'May I stroke your dog?' she asked, in a distinctly salacious fashion.

Before Lance could reply, Thunder, who was curled up at Lance's feet, snarled at her and backed away.

I really like Thunder. That dog has good taste.

I'm glad Lance didn't tell him off too badly. He picked him up, put him on his lap and told his dog that it wasn't nice to snarl at women. Especially women like Morgana. I think Lance may have regretted his action though because after that, Morgana seemed a little anxious and wouldn't get too close to Lance for the remainder of the evening. On the one or two occasions that she did, Thunder lifted his head from Lance's lap and bared his teeth at her.

I really, really like Thunder.

'I'm off to bed,' Art says, getting up suddenly and glaring at me. 'It's been a very long, and a distinctly strange day. What with all the travelling and the blizzard and everything.'

I think that last part was an afterthought and it was said for Dad's benefit, not mine, because Art was smiling sheepishly at Dad when he said it.

'Good night, Art. Sleep well.' I stay where I am but I smile at him.

'Not going with him?' Aunt Vicki says, rather unhelpfully.

'Of course not,' I say. 'This is Dad's and Bella's house. I know the rules. When in Rome, and all that.'

Aunt Vicki gives me a quelling look before bursting out laughing. Which also doesn't help.

I can see Bella's question in her eyes and I hope she can see the pleading look in mine. Obviously she does.

'We may be old-fashioned,' she says rather loudly, 'but we don't allow unmarried people to share the same room. It's one of our rules and we hope our guests will respect them. We don't have many.'

'Rules or guests?' Camilla says, looking down her nose.

'Rules,' Lance says, to my utmost astonishment. 'They don't have many rules. They have a great many guests because they're such lovely people – each and every one of them.'

'Rules?' Dad asks Bella.

'Yes, darling. Rules. Our rules. The ones we feel are most important.'

Dad stares at her for a second or two before he nods in a serious fashion. 'Yes. Yes. Very important.'

I think we're overdoing the point so try to change the subject.

'They say there'll only be one blizzard tomorrow.'

'Oh great,' Art says, and finally goes to bed.

One by one, everybody starts to drift upstairs. I hope that I may finally get a chance to speak to Lance, but it's pretty obvious that Morgana has no intention of going to bed all the while Lance is within reach. There's no point in me sitting here so I get up, say good night and head towards the door. I see Lance start to get up as if he's going to follow me but Morgana's all over him the second he puts Thunder on the floor.

'I'd better head off home,' he says, as he disentangles himself from Morgana.

'I heard Bella say you could stay the night,' Morgana says, seductively.

'Er. Yes. But I'd better go home.'

'But the weather's awful. I don't think I could sleep knowing you might be out there somewhere, driving home in this. Why don't you stay?'

'No,' he says, rather sharply for a man who seems so besotted. 'I want to go home. I like to sleep in my own bed.'

She runs her hand up his arm. 'I think I'd like to sleep in your bed, too.'

Oh dear God! I cough loudly and she turns and looks at me.

'Oh. Are you still here? I thought you'd gone to bed.'

'I can't go to bed until Lance has left. It's another one of our rules. There must always be a member of the Hall family to show our guests to the door.'

I can see she doesn't believe me but I don't care.

Lance nods and smiles. 'Yes. I've always liked that particular rule.'

Morgana sighs. 'We'll show him out together then.'

She grabs his hand possessively and leads him to the door. I follow and Thunder trots beside me. The dog's lip is curled and he's emitting a throaty little snarl. I feel like doing the same, and when Lance reaches the door and turns to say good night, and Morgana stands on tiptoed stilettos and plants a kiss on his lips, I want to do more than snarl.

Lance looks so surprised, he grabs the door knob and dashes out without saying anything. Thunder only just manages to race through the gap as the front door slams shut with a resounding bang.

Morgana looks at me and smiles. 'I always have that effect on men,' she crows. 'I like to take control. It leaves them speechless and gasping for more. You should try that on my brother. Rules, Harri, are meant to be broken.'

Chapter Thirty-Six

I would never describe The Hall as particularly large. It's big and it's got about thirty rooms, give or take, although only about ten of those are habitable, but it's not the sort of place one could ever get lost in. So imagine my astonishment when I find that in fact, if you are trying to avoid someone, or several people, The Hall is actually much larger than you might think.

Other than seeing Art and his family at breakfast this morning – which was an unusually sombre experience, even with Theo and Thor's antics... or possibly because of their antics – I've so far managed to dodge the Camlan-Browns for most of the morning.

I did have to hide in the stables for almost an hour at one stage, but I took the opportunity to groom and pet Pegasus and Sirius; even cleaning out their boxes was preferable to spending as much as ten minutes in Camilla or Morgana's company.

As for Art's dad, I think he's adopting my approach, and hiding from his wife and children. I did spot him a few times this morning, lurking in Merrion's vicinity. I'm not sure 'lurking' is quite the right word, but it sounds so much nicer than 'stalking'.

I'm still not entirely sure whether I do or don't love Art, but I am sure of one thing. There is no way I want Camilla as my mother-in-law, Morgana, as my sister-in-law and I definitely don't want Phillip as my father-in-law. For a man who's hardly said one word, frankly he gives me the creeps. What's more, from the moment they arrived they've been looking down their noses at us; as if they expected to meet Royalty and found beggars. At The Hall, as if it's a barn instead of a Palace and at me – a swan who turned out to be an ugly duckling.

They weren't even impressed by the Christmas lights.

'Oh,' Camilla said, when we switched them on last night. 'I see you've gone for multi-coloured. How terribly… quaint. And so many of them. We prefer the 'less is more' approach ourselves. And white, of course. Nothing but white.'

And when she met Theo and Thor today at breakfast, I think that was probably another treat she would rather have done without. Unbelievably, the twins were playing quietly in their room when the Camlan-Browns arrived yesterday. And thanks to Bella's precision planning, they were fed, bathed and fast asleep in bed without crossing paths with

Art's family, so the Camlan-Browns didn't lay eyes on them until this morning.

'These are *yours*?' Camilla asked, a few minutes after meeting them. 'And you're *still* going to have another? Good God! I don't know what to say.'

Ralph took the twins outside immediately after, and none of the three of them has been seen since. So I don't think I'm the only one in hiding. Or Art's dad, Phillip.

I shouldn't be in hiding though. The Hall is my home and I love it. I also love Christmas and yet since the Camlan-Browns arrived, it hasn't felt very Christmassy at all. There certainly hasn't been much goodwill and it definitely isn't very merry.

I think I need to make a stand.

I'm hungry and it's almost time for lunch, which is as good a time as any to tell them we have another rule.

Christmas at The Hall is fun. Art and his family must either join in with our Christmas festivities, or be left to their own devices while we enjoy ourselves, regardless. I wonder what Camilla will have to say about that.

Chapter Thirty-Seven

It turns out that Camilla has quite a lot to say. And none of it, what I expected.

Of course, I didn't come right out and tell her over lunch that either her family adopts a smile and gets into the Christmas spirit whether they want to or not, or they're on their own. I merely pointed out that everyone at The Hall loves Christmas and we throw ourselves into it wholeheartedly.

'As do we,' she says. 'We have *such* fun at Christmas. My husband and I are patrons of many local groups and take part in all their festivities. The women's football team. Young, women farmers. Women's rights.' She waves an arm in the air. 'Oh so many it would take all afternoon to name them. We go to all the dinner dances over the holiday period and my husband works tirelessly to support them.'

I can't help but notice the three groups she mentioned consist entirely of women. I get an uneasy feeling that the rest of them are probably similar and it makes me wonder exactly what Phillip does so 'tirelessly'.

'I am constantly asked to make appearances,' Camilla continues. 'Switching on the Christmas lights in our village – which is far larger than Hall's Cross, naturally. Book signings in the local supermarket. Talks at the village hall. Not to mention my hectic TV schedule. I hear you've become an avid fan of my show, Harriet. I'd hate you to feel intimidated in any way. I know it must be difficult when your boyfriend's mother is such a famous celebrity, but one does try to remain incognito as much as one possibly can.'

I bet *one* does.

I smile and tell her not to worry. 'If being the stepsister of a world famous, super-model hasn't intimidated me, going out with a TV celebrity's son certainly won't.'

'Lance is here,' Reece says, strolling into the kitchen. 'I told him everyone was in here except Aunt Vicki but he seemed rather eager to speak with her when I mentioned that she was alone in the sitting room.'

Morgana jumps out of her chair, nearly knocking over Camilla's glass of wine in the process.

Camilla glowers at her. 'Decorum, Morgana.' She lowers her voice. 'I thought we had discussed this. Showing one's gratitude to the man for rescuing us is one thing. But really, Morgana. *Lance?*'

She has no idea I can still hear her. Or that Merrion can.

'I don't wish to interfere Camilla,' Merrion says, as if butter wouldn't melt in her mouth. 'But considering your concerns for Harri, and not wanting her to feel intimidated, may I suggest you discourage Morgana from either seeing or being seen with Lance?'

Camilla looks startled. First, no doubt, that she may have been overheard and second, that Merrion might be an ally. 'My sentiments precisely,' she says.

Merrion nods. 'Lance may not be famous, but the media are constantly knocking at the Knightly door because of his sisters. You of course must know one of them. You're both celebrity chefs. Although I believe Ophelia is rather more well-known. And then of course, there's his younger sister, Gwen. Gwendoline Knightly-Hunter.'

Camilla blanches. 'His sisters? Knightly? Ophelia Knightly! Lance is related to Ophelia Knightly! And... and Gwendoline Knightly-Hunter? *The* Gwendoline Knightly-Hunter?'

Merrion nods again. 'Yes. He's spending Christmas with them both at Ophelia's second home in Aspen.'

Camilla's mouth is open so wide it would accommodate an entire Christmas pudding and still have room to spare. Of course, I have no idea why she's looking so stunned. Merrion told me a little about Ophelia, and so did Lance. But neither said anything much about Gwen. I can't help but wonder what Gwen has done to justify Camilla's reaction. Lance told me his younger sister was fifteen years his junior. He also told me that he's thirty-three so that makes Gwen eighteen. Why would Camilla be so in awe of an eighteen-year-old girl? Is Gwen some sort of celebrity chef, too? I want to ask but as everyone else seems to know, I decide not to show my ignorance.

It takes a while but Camilla gradually regains her composure and smiles at Morgana.

'Take no notice of me, my darling. You know how much Mummy worries. Lance is obviously a wonderful man, and so chivalrous. If you young things are smitten, far be it for me to interfere.' She smiles at Merrion, Bella and finally at me. 'Ah, love's young dream. I do wish you had told us, Harriet, that you are such good friends with the Knightlys.'

'I'm not. I only met Lance last week and I haven't met either of his sisters.'

'Oh! You will keep your little secrets.'

'I'm not keeping…' I let my voice trail off. I really can't be bothered.

And if Lance is *smitten* with Morgana, I almost feel sorry for the man.

Chapter Thirty-Eight

After lunch we all head towards the sitting room. Morgana and Camilla seem to be competing as to who will get there first, but when Morgana bursts through the doorway, she's clearly disappointed.

'If you're looking for Lance,' Aunt Vicki snaps at her. 'He's not here.'

Camilla sidles past her daughter. 'Dear Victoria. Where exactly, did that sweetheart of a man disappear to?'

'As far away from here as he can get, if he's got any sense. And he has. That man isn't stupid.'

'I didn't think for a moment that he was. I was only telling my darling Morgana, during lunch, that she could do far worse than fall for the charms of a man like that.'

'I don't doubt it.' Aunt Vicki fixes her eyes on me. 'Harriet, come here. I want to go to my room and I need your assistance.'

As Aunt Vicki has never asked for assistance in her life, I find that difficult to believe but I do as she asks.

'Of course, I'll help you, Aunt Vicki but we're all going outside to help the twins build snowmen, and to collect pine cones and cut down the trees for the Great Hall and in here. Don't you want to stay until we've done that? We'll roast chestnuts on the fire as always, and drink spiced hot chocolate. You love that.'

'Don't talk to me as if I'm five years old. I want to go to my room and I'm asking you to assist me.'

I glance at Bella, who shakes her head. Aunt Vicki can be grouchy but this is a first, even for her.

'Well, Harriet?' Aunt Vicki adds. 'Are you going to stand there all day?'

I take her arm and link it through mine and together we leave the sitting room. As I close the door behind us, she promptly removes her arm from mine and marches on ahead, turning back to look at me when she reaches the foot of the stairs.

'Come along,' she says. 'I want to get upstairs, spend a few minutes in my room and get back down in time for all the fun.'

I have no idea what's going on.

'Am I missing something?' I ask.

'Yes,' she says emphatically. 'The chance of a lifetime, unless you pull your socks up and do something about it.'

I still have no idea what's going on.

'You seem perfectly capable, as always, of getting to your room without my help. And if all you're planning to do is spend a few minutes up there, and come back down again, I really don't see why you need me.'

'I don't.'

'Then why am I here? What's going on, Aunt Vicki?'

Before she has a chance to answer, Art, who I think has been avoiding me as much as I've been avoiding him, comes dashing towards me, pulling me to him in a loving embrace. I haven't seen him since breakfast and he didn't join us for lunch.

'Harri, darling. I've been looking for you everywhere.'

'Have you? We've all been having lunch.'

'Ah. I lost track of time. Mum's just texted me to tell me. I must've missed her earlier text.'

I'm not sure why he's telling me this and Aunt Vicki glares at him.

'Harriet is assisting me to my room,' she says. 'Your mother's in the sitting room.'

'Let me help,' he offers, beaming at her.

'Harriet's helping.'

'I can help Harri.' He smiles, takes my hand firmly in his and leads me towards my aunt.

'I don't need help,' I say.

I'm now utterly bewildered. Everyone seems to be acting strangely. I hope there wasn't something in our coffee this morning. I begin to wonder if

Reece is trying out a new experiment and has failed to mention it.

'I'll simply walk with you then,' Art says. 'I need something from my room so we're heading in the same direction.'

It's only when I see Dad and Lance talking in the Long Gallery that I wonder if Aunt Vicki was setting me up. Was she going to say that she needed to ask Dad something and get me to go and get him? That would leave me alone with Lance. Or am I being completely ridiculous?

Whether she was or whether she wasn't, it's probably as clear to her as it is to me that Art will foil that plan. Despite me telling him I don't need help, he's holding my hand as if he'll never let me go. In an oddly familiar way, it's actually very comforting. It seems so strange that less than a fortnight ago, I was in Australia with Art and I was hoping he was going to propose during the Christmas holidays. We were happy together in Sydney. I thought we were in love.

What's happened to us?

What's happened to me?

Perhaps Reece has been putting something in the coffee, after all. Although I doubt that very much. If he had, at least one of us would no doubt have spontaneously combusted by now. Most of Reece's experiments end with something blowing up.

Chapter Thirty-Nine

The only thing blowing up around here at the moment is my love life.

Art's decided he doesn't want to leave my side, and Lance can't seem to take his eyes off me. Every time I glance in his direction he's looking at me with an inscrutable expression on his face.

We're all huddled in the sitting room trying to get some feeling back into our fingers, toes and other body parts, having been outside for most of the afternoon and early evening. The first hour was spent selecting the Christmas trees for the sitting room and the Great Hall. Having decided on the perfect specimens, Dad and Lance cut them down, and with ropes tied to the trunks, we all helped drag the trees back to the colonnade where they remained propped up until the snow had melted from their many branches.

Next, we went in search of pine cones, some for hanging on the trees and some to display in various antique bowls. After that, we gathered in the apple orchard, cutting bunches of mistletoe from the trees in which the festive but parasitic plants were growing, and in the woods we cut several sprays of berry-laden holly. We piled all these things into the utility room. Tonight, after dinner, we'll trim the mistletoe and holly and tie them in bunches with colourful ribbons and bows.

It was getting dark by the time we finished helping Theo and Thor build snowmen. We stood for a while, admiring the row of men and women, proudly dressed in our old scarfs and hats, their crystal-white bodies glistening in the glow of the multi-coloured lights which deck The Hall and large Christmas tree on the lawn.

By now we were all more than ready for hot chocolate by the fire – except the twins, who, somewhat inevitably, decided we should have a snowball fight. We spent a good half hour or so pelting one another with balls of compact snow, some of which felt more like balls of solid ice. Dad finally called a halt to the 'war' by declaring there was a risk of someone suffering serious injury. I think Camilla receiving a direct hit to her right cheek was the deciding factor, but Bella is almost certain the resulting black eye will heal in a day or two. And Merrion says it will hardly be noticeable beneath Camilla's skilfully applied layers of make-up.

'You'll stay for dinner won't you, Lance, and later, help us decorate the trees,' Bella says, getting up and heading for the kitchen.

'You must,' Morgana commands, draping her arm across his knee. That is until Thunder puts a stop to that with a throaty growl and a threatening snarl.

'Of course he'll stay,' Merrion says. 'He's been a part of this family tradition for the last two years.'

That statement tugs at my heartstrings for some reason. Partly I suppose because it reminds me what I've missed and partly because I wonder what Christmas was like with Lance here.

'If you're sure I'm not intruding,' Lance says, throwing an odd look in my direction.

Dad laughs. 'Of course you're not intruding, Lance. As Merrion says, we think of you as part of this family now. You're stuck with that whether you like the idea or not.'

I get to my feet and follow Bella. 'I'll help with dinner.'

Art jumps up. 'I'll help too.'

Lance looks at me as if he's about to speak but then stares into the fire and doesn't say a word.

Chapter Forty

I still can't believe it's now Friday and tomorrow will be Christmas Eve.

Last night, things didn't go quite the way they were expected. We got through dinner without too much drama although for a moment I wasn't sure we would. Theo and Thor were overtired and probably should have gone straight to bed. I know that children, no matter what their age, should not throw food across the table but I could almost see Thor's point. He thought Camilla's face might look better if her eyes matched. But flicking meatballs at her, I accept, was not the way to make that happen.

Screaming that the twins were feral beasts was, I feel, an overreaction, and understandably not a comment that would endear her to my family, but Bella didn't tell Camilla that if she didn't like it at The Hall, she was more than welcome to leave. Aunt Vicki said that for her.

Somehow, Dad and Bella managed to settle ruffled feathers and no one said one unpleasant word during dessert. Well, no one said one word at all. In fact, no one said a great deal for the rest of the evening until Merrion announced it was time to decorate the trees.

That lifted everyone's spirits, and fortified by several glasses of Aunt Vicki's Christmas Cocktail, or brandy, and champagne, we got through that process almost without a hitch. Some of us even had fun. At least the twins went to bed happy, although the same unfortunately, can't be said for Camilla. And as it happens, Thor and I were wrong. Her face doesn't look better with matching eyes, and Merrion swears she didn't know her elbow was anywhere near Camilla's head.

I can't remember much more about the evening but I do remember Art holding a bunch of mistletoe above my head before pulling me into his arms and kissing me. It was almost like old times, and I had had quite a lot to drink by then, so wrapping my arms around his neck and sinking into his kiss, seemed perfectly natural at the time. There was nothing natural about the way Morgana kissed Lance though, shortly afterwards. In fact, it looked almost obscene. But after that, as I said, my memory fails me, which is probably due to the amount of Christmas Cocktail I drank to try to block that image from my mind.

I must make sure I don't drink as much tonight. This morning I had the hangover from hell and it took some time for it to clear. I couldn't even face breakfast, but apparently nor could anyone else, and it wasn't until around eleven that Bella, Merrion, Aunt Vicki and I, began preparing for the party.

In spite of the blizzards and several feet of snow covering the ground, the 'thank you' party for Lance and his men is still going ahead. We've spent most of the day cooking, and checking that the previously cooked food which Bella had frozen and yesterday had left out to defrost, was thoroughly thawed. Large, Christmas-themed serving plates have been piled high with delicious looking fayre and displayed on the dining table and sideboards to make the perfect, festive feast.

There'll be mulled wine simmering in a large pot on the stove, and Reece has instructions to ensure every guest receives a glass of the steaming, spiced wine, upon arrival. Dad, Ralph, Reece and even Art, have been bringing cases of wine, champagne and beer up from the cellar to the utility room where the bottles will be close at hand to make sure that no one's glass will remain empty for long.

We haven't seen Lance at all today, which is probably just as well. Merrion tells me that he left about half an hour after that kiss with Morgana, and Merrion's furious with me. I know I had a lot to drink, and Merrion knows that too, but she says that's no excuse for the way I behaved. Apparently, I insisted on turning up the Christmas music playing quietly in the background last night, to full volume and dancing in the Great Hall with Art. She says it looked as if I couldn't keep my hands off Art and that was why Lance left. But as I pointed out to her,

Lance has no right to feel annoyed. He did kiss Morgana after all and has done nothing but flirt with the woman since the moment he carried her across the snow to The Hall.

To which Merrion replied: 'Sometimes, Harri, you are *really* stupid.'

Art came in and put his arms around me at that moment and since then we've all been so busy that I haven't had a chance to ask her what she meant. I'm already running late and by the time I've washed and dressed and gone back downstairs, guests have started arriving. But there's still no sign of Lance.

Morgana's looking stunning in a tightly-fitted, low-cut, silver dress. I can't help feeling slightly envious, especially of her legs. The woman has incredible legs. They're slim and long and perfectly shaped and the hem of her dress is so short that I don't think there's a part of them that isn't on display. I'd kill for legs like hers.

Camilla's make-up is so good that Merrion was right, you can hardly see her black eyes – either one of them. Philip is standing to one side of her, his eyes scanning the room like those of a child standing in front of a toy shop window, and Art is standing to the other, so deep in conversation with his mum that he doesn't notice me.

Christmas music is playing in the background and the smell of the spices in the mulled wine, is wafting in my direction.

I'm sure one glass won't hurt.

And neither will a second.

Everyone seems happy but I notice that Morgana keeps glancing towards the front doors.

As do I. I spend at least an hour socialising but every few minutes I dart a look towards those doors.

But there is still no sign of Lance.

And now, there isn't any sign of Dad. I want to ask if Lance said he would be delayed. I would ask Ralph, but there isn't any sign of him either. And now that I think of it, I haven't seen Art for a little while.

'Looking for someone?' Morgana says, from behind my left shoulder.

I turn around and manage a smile. 'I was looking for my dad. I don't suppose you've seen him lately?'

'Actually, I have. He and Art went in that direction a little while ago.' She nods her head in the direction of Dad's study. 'Art wants to ask him something, so Mum says. Art and Mum were whispering about it earlier today, but don't ask me what it is because no one in my family tells me anything.'

'I know how that feels,' I say. 'I think I'll get another drink then.'

I head towards the kitchen, wondering what Art could possibly want to ask my dad when I suddenly remember. Oh my God! I turn and run back the way I came.

I race into Dad's study, screaming, 'Stop!' at the top of my voice. 'Please don't ask Dad that question.'

Art gives me the strangest look. 'It's too late. I already have. But I didn't get the answer I was hoping for.'

Dad shakes his head. 'I'm sorry, Art. I know you think it's a fabulous idea. Perhaps I'm wrong and you're right. But I just can't agree to it.'

'Is it the money?' Art says. 'I can probably come up with some more, if that's the only sticking point.'

'It's not the money. Although it would come in handy I'll admit, and it would ease the financial situation somewhat. But I simply can't say yes.'

'What?' I interrupt their flow. Is Art actually offering to pay Dad for my hand in marriage? I ask that question outright. They both look at me as if I've completely lost my mind.

'Your hand in what?' Art queries.

'Marriage?' Dad says. 'Who said anything about marriage? Are you two getting married?'

'No,' Art says, a little too quickly.

'Oh,' says Dad. 'Because if you were, that might put an entirely different light on the matter.'

Art looks excited. 'You mean, if Harri and I get engaged you'd consider my proposal?'

Dad nods. 'I'd certainly give it a great deal of thought. And if it's what Harri wants, of course that changes everything. I'd probably agree. Although I'd have to discuss it with Bella.'

'Then let's get engaged.' Art turns and beams at me. 'It's not such a bad idea. And we can probably work that into the schedule too. Mum could pretend to do the catering. That would work.'

I look from one to the other. 'What are you talking about? Haven't you already asked Dad if you can marry me?'

Art looks bewildered. 'No. I said I hadn't.'

'Then... what have you asked him?'

'I asked if we can use The Hall to film a new series of Mum's cooking show. It's going to be called, *Country Cooking in an English Stately Home with Camilla Camlan-Brown* and I'm coming home to produce it. We were originally planning a series called *Cooking at Hall Castle with Camilla Camlan-Brown* but when we saw The Hall, we realised that was a non-starter. There is no way we could pass this place off as anything like Highclere Castle. I know you said it had seen better days, but we didn't expect it to look like this, and it seemed much larger in the photos. Anyway, we had a total rethink and came up with the new idea. It's a little more downmarket but we're sure we can still pull in the viewers. And, as I said to your dad, we can knock down a few walls, put up a false façade, and the place will look like an English stately home should look.'

I can't believe what I'm hearing. I really can't. It just goes to show that sometimes when you think you know someone, you really don't know them at all. No wonder Art wanted to keep his 'little secret'.

He knew I wouldn't agree. He knows how I feel about having strangers wandering around The Hall when they come to see the Tudor kitchen and that's only a few times a year. He obviously thought he'd have more luck going directly to Dad.

'So let's get engaged, Harri,' Art says. 'I'll go and tell Mum, and we'll organise the schedule. The sooner we get things moving, the better.'

'Er. No. No way. I'm not completely sure I know what's going on here, but I am sure of one thing. I don't want to marry you, Art.'

He looks a tad annoyed, but then he shrugs. 'Okay. We'll discuss the marriage stuff later. We just have to get engaged for now.'

'No!' I shriek. 'You're not listening. There's nothing to discuss. I'm not going to marry you so there's no point in getting engaged to you. Not today. Not tomorrow. Not ever.'

'That's a bit harsh.'

'I'm sorry. But it's the truth.'

'So… you just want to carry on as we are?' He looks at Dad. 'Surely we can work something out?'

'I don't think we can,' Dad says, giving me an odd sort of smile.

'But we'll still be living together,' Art says, looking from Dad to me and back to Dad again.

'I don't think you will,' Dad says. 'Unless I'm very much mistaken, I think my wonderful daughter has fallen in love with someone else.'

Art looks at me in disbelief.

I smile at Dad, and nod. 'I'm sorry, Art. Dad's right. I have fallen in love with someone else. Deeply in love. And there's not a thing I can do about it.'

'Damn,' Art says. 'I suppose that means we'll have to find somewhere else to film Mum's new series.'

'Yes,' Dad says, 'I rather think it does. And may I suggest that the sooner you get on with that, the better.'

Art looks at me as if it's finally sinking in. 'I suppose that also means our relationship is over.'

I nod. 'Yes, Art. It absolutely does.'

Chapter Forty-One

It's Christmas Eve evening and I'm standing in the Long Gallery looking out onto a vista that would make the perfect Christmas card scene. As far as the eye can see, the trees and bushes all wear coats of white, and gently falling snowflakes are drifting towards the crisp, white blanket still covering the ground. The multi-coloured Christmas lights cast a kaleidoscope of colours on the crystal-like snow. There's hardly any moon tonight, but a faint shaft of light beams through the windows of the Long Gallery and sprinkles silver moon dust on the polished oak floor. It's the perfect setting for romance. But unfortunately, I'm here alone.

I'm not entirely alone, of course. All of my family are downstairs celebrating, but Art and his family have left. It seemed they'd rather drive through snow and ice than spend Christmas at The Hall and now that it's over between me and Art, there wasn't much point in them staying.

I'll go back downstairs soon and we'll start opening presents. We always open two each on Christmas Eve. It's a tradition. So are the mince pies we'll eat and the egg nog we'll drink while we're handing out the gifts. I just needed a moment alone. Some time to think about what I've lost. And what I've let slip away.

Losing Art isn't really a loss. I thought we were in love but we weren't and once I realised that, there was really no point in dragging things out. Love can be deceiving and it's only when the real thing presents itself that we realise what we thought was love wasn't love at all. Not real love. Not the kind of love I felt for Lance... feel for Lance.

Merrion, Ralph and Bella all say I shouldn't worry, and so does Dad. That Lance will come back. That when he does, they're sure he'll tell me he feels the same way about me. But how can I be sure? How can they be sure? We'll just have to wait and see. They may be right. I hope they are. Merrion said when I first arrived that this Christmas wouldn't turn out as I expected, and she was definitely right about that. So all I can do is hope. Hope that Lance will come back and hope that when he does, he'll tell me he loves me as much as I know I love him.

I breathe onto the glass and draw the outline of a heart. Inside I write my name and his with the words 'True Love' beneath. It's a childish thing to do, I know, but it makes me smile.

'I thought your name was Harri with an 'i', not Harry with a 'y' and only Harriet to Vicki – and people you don't like.'

Lance's deep, and oh so sexy voice interrupts my thoughts, but I know I am imagining it. He's in Aspen with his sisters so I know it can't be him. He wasn't due to fly out until today but apparently he changed his flight and flew out yesterday. That's why he wasn't at the party here last night.

'I've flown thousands of miles to be here, and flying terrifies me. Won't you at least look at me?'

I didn't imagine that.

I spin round on the spot and there he is. Standing in the doorway, that tell-tale twitch at the corner of his mouth and something in his eyes I can't quite see clearly in this light but that sends a thrill of excitement pulsing through me. I want to run to him, but I mustn't. I still don't know if he likes me. Despite what Merrion and Ralph have said.

'I thought you were in Aspen. Ralph told me you left yesterday.'

Lance nods and takes a step towards me. 'I did. Now I'm back. Although I only got as far as Denver.'

I can't believe this. I really can't.

'But… you're terrified of flying. We were all surprised you actually got on the plane and left. To be here now you must have got on another plane straight back.'

'Two planes. There were no direct flights to get me here in time. But I managed to stop long enough to have a gingerbread latte at Denver airport with my sisters. They were the ones who sorted out the flights to get me back. I didn't think I could make it but anything is possible when my sisters put their minds to it. And now I'm here. And you're still over there. Why is that, exactly? I was hoping you'd rush into my arms the moment I said your name. But I suppose a man can only dream.'

I *really* can't believe this. I beam at him but force myself to stay exactly where I am.

'Why should I run to you? You were the one who left. And you didn't even say goodbye.'

'That's true.'

'I'm not even sure if you like me. You've never said you do. You've never tried to kiss me. In fact, you've always been the one to walk away.'

'You told me you loved your boyfriend. That you were expecting – and hoping he was coming here to propose. I didn't want to be a quick 'hook up'. Nothing more than a holiday fling.'

'It looked like you were more than willing to have a fling with Morgana.'

'I wasn't in the least bit interested in Morgana.'

'You kissed her.'

'She kissed me. It took me by surprise. And I was struggling to cope with seeing you and Art together.'

'That's why you left?'

'That's why I left. But Ralph phoned and told me you and Art are history. Unfortunately I didn't get his message until I landed in Denver so there wasn't much I could do. But now I'm back, and there is. I've come to ask if you'll have dinner with me. To go out on a date.'

'I'll have to check my busy schedule but I think I can squeeze you in. I assume that does mean you like me then?'

He grins. 'Harriet. It was difficult enough for me to get on a plane the first time and it wasn't a pleasant experience, so believe me, the only reason I got back onto the very next plane I could, and the plane after that, *was* because I like you. I like you a lot. And the thought of spending Christmas with you was much stronger than my fear of flying. Even my sisters understood.'

I'm so happy I could scream.

He's smiling, but he's walking far too slowly for my liking.

I run to him and throw myself into his open arms and when he kisses me, I feel as if I'm in one of Reece's experiments. My insides turn to goo and my blood is definitely bubbling through my veins. I'm tingling from head to toe and as Lance pulls me closer and kisses me deeper, I can tell he feels the same.

I just hope we don't both explode.

THE END

MERRY CHRISTMAS!

Thank you for reading, *Deck the Halls.* I hope you enjoyed it and if so, I would absolutely love it if you would consider telling your friends and/or posting a short review on Amazon. Word of mouth is an author's best friend and very much appreciated. Thanks so much.

To see details of my other books, please go to the books page on my website or scan the QR code, below. www.emilyharvale.com/books.

***

Scan the code above to see Emily's books on Amazon

To read about me, my books, my work in progress and competitions, freebies, or to contact me, pop over to my website www.emilyharvale.com. To be the first to hear about new releases and other news, you can subscribe to my Readers' Club newsletter via the 'Sign me up' box.

Or why not come and say 'Hello' on Facebook, Twitter, Instagram or Pinterest. Hope to chat with you soon.

63822720R00151

Made in the USA
Charleston, SC
13 November 2016